The
Monster Maker
and
Other Stories

by

W. C. Morrow

Contents

The Monster Maker

A young man of refined appearance, but evidently suffering great mental distress, presented himself one morning at the residence of a singular old man, who was known as a surgeon of remarkable skill. The house was a queer and primitive brick affair, entirely out of date, and tolerable only in the decayed part of the city in which it stood. It was large, gloomy, and dark, and had long corridors and dismal rooms; and it was absurdly large for the small family – man and wife – that occupied it. The house described, the man is portrayed – but not the woman. He could be agreeable on occasion, but, for all that, he was but animated mystery. His wife was weak, wan, reticent, evidently miserable, and possibly living a life of dread or horror – perhaps witness of repulsive things, subject of anxieties, and victim of fear and tyranny; but there is a great deal of guessing in these assumptions. He was about sixty-five years of age and she about forty. He was lean, tall, and bald, with thin, smooth-shaven face, and very keen eyes; kept always at home, and was slovenly. The man was strong, the woman weak; he dominated, she suffered.

Although he was a surgeon of rare skill, his practice was almost nothing, for it was a rare occurrence that the few who knew of his great ability were brave enough to penetrate the gloom of his house, and when they did so it was with deaf ear turned to sundry ghoulish stories that were whispered concerning him. These were, in great part, but exaggerations of his experiments in vivisection; he was devoted to the science of surgery.

The young man who presented himself on the morning just mentioned was a handsome fellow, yet of evident weak character and unhealthy temperament – sensitive, and easily exalted or depressed. A single glance convinced the surgeon that his visitor was seriously affected in mind, for there was never bolder skull-grin of melancholia, fixed and irremediable.

A stranger would not have suspected any occupancy of the house The street door – old, warped, and blistered by the sun – was locked, and the small, faded-green window-blinds were closed. The young man rapped at the door. No answer. He rapped again. Still no sign. He examined a slip of paper, glanced at the number of the house, and then, with the impatience of a child, he furiously kicked the door. There were signs of numerous other such kicks. A response came in the shape of a shuffling footstep in the hail, a turning of the rusty key, and a sharp face that peered through a cautious opening in the door.

"Are you the doctor?" asked the young man.

"Yes, yes! Come in," briskly replied the master of the house.

The young man entered. The old surgeon closed the door and carefully locked it. "This way, " he said, advancing to a rickety flight of stairs. The young man followed. The surgeon led the way up the stairs, turned into a narrow, musty-smelling corridor at the left, traversed it, rattling the loose boards under his feet, at the farther end opened a door at the right, and beckoned his visitor to enter. The young man found himself in a pleasant room, furnished in antique fashion and with hard simplicity.

"Sit down," said the old man, placing a chair so that its occupant should face a window that looked out upon a dead wall about six feet from the house. He threw open the blind, and a pale light entered. He then seated himself near his visitor and directly facing him, and with a searching look, that had all the power of a microscope, he proceeded to diagnosticate the case.

"Well?" he presently asked. The young man shifted uneasily in his seat.

"I – I have come to see you," he finally stammered, "because I'm in trouble."

"Ah!"

"Yes; you see, I – that is – I have given it up."

"Ah!" There was pity added to sympathy in the ejaculation.

"That's it. Given it up," added the visitor. He took from his pocket a role of banknotes, and with the utmost deliberation he counted them out upon his knee. "Five thousand dollars," he calmly remarked. "That is for you. It's all I have; but I presume – I imagine – no; that is not the word – *assume* – yes; that's the word – assume that five thousand – is it really that much? Let me count." He counted again. "That five thousand dollars is a sufficient fee for what I want you to do."

The surgeon's lips curled pityingly – perhaps disdainfully also. "What do you want me to do?" he carelessly inquired.

The young man rose, looked around with a mysterious air, approached the surgeon, and laid the money across his knee. Then he stopped and whispered two words in the surgeon's ear.

These words produced an electric effect. The old man started violently; then, springing to his feet, he caught his visitor angrily, and transfixed him with a look that was as sharp as a knife. His eyes flashed, and he opened his mouth to give utterance to some harsh imprecation, when he suddenly checked himself. The anger left his face, and only pity remained. He relinquished his grasp, picked up the scattered notes, and, offering them to the visitor, slowly said:

"I do not want your money. You are simply foolish. You think you are in trouble. Well, you do not know what trouble is. Your only trouble is that you have not a trace of manhood in your nature. You are merely insane – I shall not say pusillanimous. You should surrender yourself to the authorities, and be sent to a lunatic asylum for proper treatment."

The young man keenly felt the intended insult, and his eyes flashed dangerously.

"You old dog – you insult me thus!" he cried. "Grand airs, these, you give yourself! Virtuously indignant, old murderer, you! Don't want my money, eh? When a man comes to you himself and wants it done, you may fly into a passion and spurn his money; but let an enemy of his come and pay you, and you are only too willing. How many such jobs have you done in this miserable old hole? It is a good thing for you that the police have not run you down, and brought spade and shovel with them. Do you know what is said of you? Do you think you have kept your windows so closely shut that no sound has ever penetrated beyond them? Where do you keep your infernal implements?"

He had worked himself into a high passion. His voice was hoarse, loud, and rasping. His eyes, bloodshot, started from their sockets. His whole frame twitched, and his fingers writhed. But he was in the presence of a man infinitely his superior. Two eyes, like those of a snake, burned two holes through him. An overmastering, inflexible presence confronted one weak and passionate.

The result came.

"Sit down," commanded the stem voice of the surgeon.

It was the voice of father to child, of master to slave. The fury left the visitor, who, weak and overcome, fell upon a chair.

Meanwhile, a peculiar light had appeared in the old surgeon's face, the dawn of a strange idea; a gloomy ray, strayed from the fires of the bottomless pit; the baleful light that illumines the way of the enthusiast. The old man remained a moment in profound abstraction, gleams of eager intelligence bursting momentarily through the cloud of somber meditation that covered his face.

Then broke the broad light of a deep, impenetrable determination. There was something sinister in it, suggesting the sacrifice of something held sacred. After a struggle, mind had vanquished conscience.

Taking a piece of paper and a pencil, the surgeon carefully wrote answers to questions which he peremptorily addressed to his visitor, such as his name, age, place of residence, occupation, and the like, and the same inquiries concerning his parents, together with other particular matters.

"Does anyone know you came to this house?" he asked.

"No."

"You swear it?"

"Yes."

"But your prolonged absence will cause alarm and lead to search."

"I have provided against that."

"How?"

"By depositing a note in the post, as I came along, announcing my intention to drown myself."

"The river will be dragged."

"What then?" asked the young man, shrugging his shoulders with careless indifference. "Rapid undercurrent, you know. A good many are never found."

There was a pause.

"Are you ready?" finally asked the surgeon.

"Perfectly." The answer was cool and determined.

The manner of the surgeon, however, showed much perturbation. The pallor that had come into his face at the moment his decision was formed became intense. A nervous tremulousness overcame his frame. Above it shone the light of enthusiasm.

"Have you a choice in the method?" he asked.

"Yes; extreme anesthesia."

"With what agent?"

"The surest and quickest."

"Do you desire any – any subsequent disposition?"

"No; only nullification; simply a blowing out, as of a candle in the wind; a puff – then darkness, without a trace. A sense of your own safety may suggest the method. I leave it to you."

"No delivery to your friends?"

"None whatever."

Another pause.

"Did you say you are quite ready?" asked the surgeon.

"Quite ready."

"And perfectly willing?"

"Anxious."

"Then wait a moment."

With this request the old surgeon rose to his feet and stretched himself. Then with the stealthiness of a cat he opened the door and peered into the hall, listening intently. There was no sound. He softly closed the door and locked it. Then he closed the window-blinds and locked them. This done, he opened a door leading into an adjoining room, which, though it had no window, was lighted by means of a small skylight. The young man watched closely. A strange change had come over him. While his determination had not one whit lessened, a look of great relief came into his face, displacing the haggard, despairing look of a half-hour before.

Melancholic then, he was ecstatic now.

The opening of a second door disclosed a curious sight. In the centre of the room, directly under the skylight, was an operating-table, such as is used by demonstrators of anatomy. A glass case against the wall held surgical instruments of every kind. Hanging in another case were human skeletons of various sizes. In sealed jars, arranged on shelves, were monstrosities of divers kinds preserved in alcohol. There were also, among innumerable other articles scattered about the room, a manikin, a stuffed cat, a desiccated human heart, plaster casts of various parts of the body, numerous charts, and a large assortment of drugs and chemicals. There was also a lounge, which could be opened to form a couch. The surgeon opened it and moved the operating-table aside, giving its place to the lounge.

"Come in," he called to his visitor.

The young man obeyed without the least hesitation.

"Take off your coat."

He complied.

"Lie down on that lounge."

In a moment the young man was stretched at full length, eyeing the surgeon. The latter undoubtedly was suffering under great excitement, but he did not waver; his movements were sure and quick. Selecting a bottle containing a liquid, he carefully measured out a certain quantity. While doing this he asked:

"Have you ever had any irregularity of the heart?"

"No."

The answer was prompt, but it was immediately followed by a quizzical look in the speaker's face.

"I presume," he added, "you mean by your question that it might be dangerous to give me a certain drug. Under the circumstances, however, I fail to see any relevancy in your question."

This took the surgeon aback; but he hastened to explain that he did not wish to inflict unnecessary pain, and hence his question.

He placed the glass on a stand, approached his visitor, and carefully examined his pulse.

"Wonderful!" he exclaimed.

"Why?"

"It is perfectly normal."

"Because I am wholly resigned. Indeed, it has been long since I knew such happiness. It is not active, but infinitely sweet."

"You have no lingering desire to retract?"

"None whatever."

The surgeon went to the stand and returned with the draught.

"Take this." he said kindly.

The young man partially raised himself and took the glass in his hand. He did not show the vibration of a single nerve. He drank the liquid, draining the last drop. Then he returned the glass with a smile.

"Thank you," he said; "you are the noblest man that lives. May you always prosper and be happy! You are my benefactor, my liberator. Bless you, bless you! You reach down from your seat with the gods and lift me up into glorious peace and rest. I love you – I love you with all my heart!"

These words, spoken earnestly, in a musical, low voice, and accompanied with a smile of ineffable tenderness, pierced the old man's heart. A suppressed convulsion swept over him; intense anguish wrung his vitals; perspiration trickled down his face. The young man continued to smile.

"Ah, it does me good!" said he.

The surgeon, with a strong effort to control himself, sat down upon the edge of the lounge and took his visitor's wrist, counting the pulse "How long will it take?" the young man asked.

"Ten minutes. Two have passed." The voice was hoarse.

"Ah, only eight minutes more!... Delicious, delicious! I feel it coming... What was that? Ah, I understand. Music... Beautiful!... Coming, coming... Is that – that – water?... Trickling? Dripping? Doctor!"

"Well?"

"Thank you... thank you... Noble man,... my savior,... my bene... bene... factor... trickling,... trickling... Dripping, dripping... Doctor!"

"Well?"

"Doctor!"

"Past hearing," muttered the surgeon.

"Doctor!"

"And blind."

Response was made by a firm grasp of the hand.

"Doctor!"

"And numb."

"Doctor!"

The old man watched and waited.

"Dripping,... dripping."

The last drop had run. There was a sigh, and nothing more.

The surgeon laid down the hand.

"The first step," he groaned, rising to his feet; then his whole frame dilated. "The first step is the most difficult, yet the simplest. A providential delivery into my hands of that for which I have hungered for forty years. No withdrawal now! It is possible, because scientific; rational, but perilous. If I succeed – *if*? I *shall* succeed. I *will* succeed... And after success – what?... Yes, what? Publish the plan and the result? The gallows... So long as *it* shall exist... and *I* exist, the gallows. That much... But how account for its presence? Ah, that pinches hard! I must trust to the future."

He tore himself from the reverie and started.

"I wonder if *she* heard or saw anything."

With that reflection he cast a glance upon the form on the lounge, and then left the room, locked the door, locked also the door of the outer room, walked down two or three corridors, penetrated to a remote part of the house, and rapped at a door. It was opened by his wife. He, by this time, had regained complete mastery over himself.

"I thought I heard some one in the house just now," he said, "but I can find no one."

"I heard nothing."

He was greatly relieved.

"I did hear some one knock at the door less than an hour ago," she resumed, "and heard you speak, I think. Did he come in?"

"No."

The woman glanced at his feet and seemed perplexed.

"I am almost certain," she said, "that I heard foot-falls in the house, and yet I see that you are wearing slippers."

"Oh, I had on my shoes then!"

"That explains it," said the woman, satisfied; "I think the sound you heard must have been caused by rats."

"Ah, that was it!" exclaimed the surgeon. Leaving, he closed the door, reopened it, and said, "I do not wish to be disturbed today." He said to himself, as he went down the hall, "All is clear there."

He returned to the room in which his visitor lay, and made a careful examination.

"Splendid specimen!" he softly exclaimed; "every organ sound; every function perfect; fine, large frame; well-shaped muscles, strong and sinewy; capable of wonderful development – if given opportunity… I have no doubt it can be done. Already I have succeeded with a dog – a task less difficult than this, for in a man the cerebrum overlaps the cerebellum, which is not the case with a dog. This gives a wide range for accident, with but one opportunity in a lifetime! In the cerebrum, the intellect and the affections; in the cerebellum, the senses and the motor forces; in the medulla oblongata, control of the diaphragm. In these two latter lie all the essentials of simple existence. The cerebrum is merely an adornment; that is to say, reason and the affections are almost purely ornamental. I have already proved it. My dog, with its cerebrum removed, was idiotic, but it retained its physical senses to a certain degree."

While thus ruminating he made careful preparations. He moved the couch, replaced the operating-table under the skylight, selected a number of surgical instruments, prepared certain drug mixtures, and arranged water, towels, and all the accessories of a tedious surgical operation.

Suddenly he burst into laughter.

"Poor fool!" he exclaimed. "Paid me five thousand dollars to kill him! Didn't have the courage to snuff his own candle! Singular, singular, the queer freaks these madmen have! You thought you were dying, poor idiot! Allow me to inform you, sir, that you are as much alive at this moment as ever you were in your life. But it will be all the same to you. You shall never be more conscious than you are now; and for all practical purposes, so far as they concern you, you are dead henceforth, though you shall live. By the way, how should you feel without a head? Ha, ha, ha… But that's a sorry joke."

He lifted the unconscious form from the lounge and laid it upon the operating table.

* * * * *

About three years afterwards the following conversation was held between a captain of police and a detective:

"She may be insane," suggested the captain.

"I think she is."

"And yet you credit her story!"

"I do."

"Singular!"

"Not at all. I myself have learned something."

"What!"

"Much, in one sense; little, in another. You have heard those queer stories of her husband. Well, they are all nonsensical – probably with one exception. He is generally a harmless old fellow, but peculiar. He has performed some wonderful surgical operations. The people in his neighborhood are ignorant, and they fear him and wish to be rid of him; hence they tell a great many lies about him, and they come to believe their own stories. The one important thing that I have learned is that he is almost insanely enthusiastic on the subject of surgery – especially experimental surgery; and with an enthusiast there is hardly such a thing as a scruple. It is this that gives me confidence in the woman's story."

"You say she appeared to be frightened?"

"Doubly so – first, she feared that her husband would learn of her betrayal of him; second, the discovery itself had terrified her."

"But her report of this discovery is very vague," argued the captain. "He conceals everything from her. She is merely guessing."

"In part – yes; in other part – no. She heard the sounds distinctly, though she did not see clearly. Horror closed her eyes. What she thinks she saw is, I admit, preposterous; but she undoubtedly saw something extremely frightful. There are many peculiar little circumstances. He has eaten with her but few times during the last three years, and nearly always carries his food to his private rooms. She says that he either consumes an enormous quantity, throws much away, or is feeding something that eats prodigiously. He explains this to her by saying that he has animals with which he experiments. This is not true. Again, he always keeps the door to these rooms carefully locked; and not only that, but he has had the doors doubled and otherwise strengthened, and has heavily barred a window that looks from one of the rooms upon a dead wall a few feet distant."

"What does it mean?" asked the captain.

"A prison."

"For animals, perhaps."

"Certainly not."

"Why!"

"Because, in the first place, cages would have been better; in the second place, the security that he has provided is infinitely greater than that required for the confinement of ordinary animals."

"All this is easily explained: he has a violent lunatic under treatment."

"I had thought of that, but such is not the fact."

"How do you know?"

"By reasoning thus: He has always refused to treat cases of lunacy; he confines himself to surgery: the walls are not padded, for the woman has heard sharp blows upon them; no human strength, however morbid, could possibly require such resisting strength as has been provided; he would not be likely to conceal a lunatic's confinement from the woman; no lunatic could consume all the food that he provides; so extremely violent mania as these precautions indicate could not continue three years; if there is a lunatic in the case it is very probable that there should have been communication with some one outside concerning the patient, and there has been none; the woman has listened at the keyhole and has heard no human voice within: and last, we have heard the woman's vague description of what she saw."

"You have destroyed every possible theory," said the captain, deeply interested, "and have suggested nothing new."

"Unfortunately, I cannot; but the truth may be very simple, after all. The old surgeon is so peculiar that I am prepared to discover something remarkable."

"Have you suspicions?"

"I have."

"Of what?" "A crime. The woman suspects it."

"And betrays it?"

"Certainly, because it is so horrible that her humanity revolts; so terrible that her whole nature demands of her that she hand over the criminal to the law; so frightful that she is in mortal terror; so awful that it has shaken her mind."

"What do you propose to do?" asked the captain.

"Secure evidence. I may need help."

"You shall have all the men you require. Go ahead, but be careful. You are on dangerous ground. You would be a mere plaything in the hands of that man."

Two days afterwards the detective again sought the captain.

"I have a queer document," he said, exhibiting torn fragments of paper, on which there was writing. "The woman stole it and brought it to me. She snatched a handful out of a book, getting only a part of each of a few leaves."

These fragments, which the men arranged as best they could, were (the detective explained) torn by the surgeon's wife from the first volume of a number of manuscript books which her husband had writ-ten on one subject, – the very one that was the cause of her excitement. "About the time that he began a certain experiment three years ago," continued the detective, "he removed everything from the suite of two rooms containing his study and his operating-room. In one of the bookcases that he removed to a room across the passage was a drawer, which he kept locked, but which he opened from time to time. As is quite common with such pieces of furniture, the lock of the drawer is a very poor one; and so the woman, while making a thorough search yesterday, found a key on her bunch that fitted this lock. She opened the drawer, drew out the bottom book of a pile (so that its mutilation would more likely escape discovery), saw that it might contain a clew, and tore out a handful of the leaves. She had barely replaced the book, locked the drawer, and made her escape when her husband appeared. He hardly ever allows her to be out of his sight when she is in that part of the house."

The fragments read as follows: "…the motory nerves. I had hardly dared to hope for such a result, although inductive reasoning had convinced me of its possibility, my only doubt having been on the score of my lack of skill. Their operation has been only slightly impaired, and even this would not have been the case had the operation been performed in infancy, before the intellect had sought and obtained recognition as an essential part of the whole. Therefore I state, as a proved fact, that the cells of the motory nerves have inherent forces sufficient to the purposes of those nerves. But hardly so with the sensory nerves. These latter are, in fact, an offshoot of the former, evolved from them by natural (though not essential) heterogeneity, and to a certain extent are dependent on the evolution and expansion of a contemporaneous tendency, that developed into mentality, or mental function. Both of these latter tendencies, these evolvements, are merely refinements of the motory system, and not independent entities; that is to say, they are blossoms of a plant that propagates from its roots. The motory system is the first.

"…nor am I surprised that such prodigious muscular energy is developing. It promises yet to surpass the wildest dreams of human strength. I account for it thus: the powers of assimilation had reached their full development. They had formed the habit of doing a certain amount of work. They sent their product to all parts of the system. As a result of my operation the consumption of these products was reduced fully one-half; that is to say, about one-half of the demand for them was withdrawn. But force of habit required the production to proceed. This production was strength, vitality, energy. Thus double the usual quantity of this strength, this energy, was stored in the remaining… developed a tendency that did surprise me. Nature, no longer suffering the distraction of extraneous interferences, and at the same time being cut in two (as it were), with reference to this case, did not fully adjust herself to the new situation, as does a magnet, which, when divided at the point of equilibrium, renews itself in its two fragments by investing each with opposite poles; but, on the contrary, being severed from laws that theretofore had controlled her, and possessing still that mysterious tendency to develop into something more potential and complex, she blindly (having lost her lantern) pushed her demands for material that would secure this development, and as blindly used it when it was given her. Hence this marvelous voracity, this insatiable hunger, this wonderful ravenousness; and hence also (there being nothing but the physical part to receive this vast storing of energy) this strength that is becoming almost hourly Herculean, almost daily appalling. It is becoming a serious... narrow escape today. By some means, while I was absent, it unscrewed the stopper of the silver feeding-pipe (which I have already herein termed 'the artificial mouth'), and in one of its curious antics, allowed all the chyle to escape from its stomach through the tube. Its hunger then became intense – I may say furious. I placed my hands upon it to push it into a chair, when, feeling my touch, it caught me, clasped me around the neck, and would have crushed me to death instantly had I not slipped from its powerful grasp. Thus I always had to be on my guard. I have provided the screw stopper with a spring catch, and usually docile when not hungry; slow and heavy in its movements, which are, of course, purely unconscious: any apparent excitement in movement being due to local irregularities in the blood-supply of the cerebellum, which, if I did not have it enclosed in a silver case that is immovable, I should expose and – "

The captain looked at the detective with a puzzled air.

"I don't understand it all," said he.

"Nor I," agreed the detective. "What do you propose to do?"

"Make a raid."

"Do you want a man?"

"Three. The strongest men in your district."

"Why, the surgeon is old and weak!"

"Nevertheless, I want three strong men; and for that matter, prudence really advises me to take twenty."

♦ ♦ ♦ ♦ ♦

At one o'clock the next morning a cautious, scratching sound might have been heard in the ceiling of the surgeon's operating-room. Shortly afterwards the skylight sash was carefully raised and laid aside. A man peered into the opening. Nothing could be heard.

"That is singular," thought the detective.

He cautiously lowered himself to the floor by a rope, and then stood for some moments listening intently. There was a dead silence. He shot the slide of a dark-lantern, and rapidly swept the room with the light. It was bare, with the exception of a strong iron staple and ring, screwed to the floor in the centre of the room, with a heavy chain attached. The detective then turned his attention to the outer room; it was perfectly bare. He was deeply perplexed. Returning to the inner room, he called softly to the men to descend. While they were thus occupied he re-entered the outer room and examined the door. A glance sufficed. It was kept closed by a spring attachment, and was locked with a strong spring-lock that could be drawn from the inside.

"The bird has just flown," mused the detective. "A singular accident! The discovery and proper use of this thumb-bolt might not have happened once in fifty years, if my theory is correct." By this time the men were behind him. He noiselessly drew the spring-bolt, opened the door, and looked out into the hall. He heard a peculiar sound. It was as though a gigantic lobster was floundering and scrambling in some distant part of the old house. Accompanying this sound was a loud, whistling breathing, and frequent rasping gasps.

These sounds were heard by still an other person, the surgeon's wife; for they originated very near her rooms, which were a considerable distance from her husband's. She had been sleeping lightly, tortured by fear and harassed by frightful dreams. The conspiracy into which she had recently entered, for the destruction of her husband, was a source of great anxiety. She constantly suffered from the most gloomy forebodings, and lived in an atmosphere of terror. Added to the natural horror of her situation were those countless sources of fear which a fright-shaken mind creates and then magnifies. She was, indeed, in a pitiable suite, having been driven first by terror to desperation, and then to madness.

Startled thus out of fitful slumber by the noise at her door, she sprang from her bed to the floor, every terror that lurked in her acutely tense in mind and diseased imagination starting up and almost overwhelming her. The idea of flight – one of the strongest of all instincts – seized upon her, and she ran to the door, beyond all control of reason. She drew the bolt and flung the door wide open, and then fled wildly down the passage, the appalling hissing and rasping gurgle ringing in her ears apparently with a thousandfold intensity. But the passage was in absolute darkness, and she had not taken a half-dozen steps when she tripped upon an unseen object on the floor. She fell headlong upon it, encountering in it a large, soft, warm substance that writhed and squirmed, and from which came the sounds that had awakened her. Instantly realizing her situation, she uttered a shriek such as only an unnamable terror can inspire. But hardly had her cry started the echoes in the empty corridor when it was suddenly stifled. Two prodigious arms had closed upon her and crushed the life out of her.

The cry performed the office of directing the detective and his assistants, and it also aroused the old surgeon, who occupied rooms between the officers and the objects of their search. The cry of agony pierced him to the marrow, and a realization of the cause of it burst upon him with frightful force.

"It has come at last!" he gasped, springing from his bed.

Snatching from a table a dimly-burning lamp and a long knife which he had kept at hand for three years, he dashed into the corridor. The four officers had already started forward, but when they saw him emerge they halted in silence. In that moment of stillness the surgeon paused to listen. He heard the hissing sound and the clumsy floundering of a bulky, living object in the direction of his wife's apartments. It evidently was advancing towards him. A turn in the corridor shut out the view. He turned up the light, which revealed a ghastly pallor in his face.

"Wife!" he called.

There was no response. He hurriedly advanced, the four men following quietly. He turned the angle of the corridor, and ran so rapidly that by the time the officers had come in sight of him again he was twenty steps away. He ran past a huge, shapeless object, sprawling, crawling, and floundering along, and arrived at the body of his wife.

He gave one horrified glance at her face, and staggered away. Then a fury seized him.

Clutching the knife firmly, and holding the lamp aloft, he sprang toward the ungainly object in the corridor. It was then that the officers, still advancing cautiously, saw a little more clearly, though still indistinctly, the object of the surgeon's fury, and the cause of the look of unutterable anguish in his face. The hideous sight caused them to pause. They saw what appeared to be a man, yet evidently was not a man; huge, awkward, shapeless; a squirming, lurching, stumbling mass, completely naked. It raised its broad shoulders. It had no head, but instead of it a small metallic ball surmounting its massive neck.

"Devil!" exclaimed the surgeon, raising the knife.

"Hold, there!" commanded a stern voice.

The surgeon quickly raised his eyes and saw the four officers, and for a moment fear paralyzed his arm.

"The police!" he gasped.

Then, with a look of redoubled fury, he sent the knife to the hilt into the squirming mass before him. The wounded monster sprang to its feet and wildly threw its arms about, meanwhile emitting fearful sounds from a silver tube through which it breathed. The surgeon aimed another blow, but never gave it. In his blind fury he lost his caution, and was caught in an iron grasp. The struggling threw the lamp some feet toward the officers, and it fell to the floor, shattered to pieces. Simultaneously with the crash the oil took fire, and the corridor was filled with flame.

The officers could not approach. Before them was the spreading blaze, and secure behind it were two forms struggling in a fearful embrace. They heard cries and gasps, and saw the gleaming of a knife.

The wood in the house was old and dry. It took fire at once, and the flames spread with great rapidity. The four officers turned and fled, barely escaping with their lives. In an hour nothing remained of the mysterious old house and its inmates but a blackened ruin.

His Unconquerable Enemy

I was summoned from Calcutta to the heart of India to perform a difficult surgical operation on one of the women of a great rajah's household. I found the rajah a man of a noble character, but possessed, as I afterward discovered, of a sense of cruelty purely Oriental and in contrast to the indolence of his disposition. He was so grateful for the success that attended my mission that he urged me to remain a guest at the palace as long as it might please me to stay, and I thankfully accepted the invitation.

One of the male servants attracted my notice for his marvelous capacity of malice. His name was Neranya, and I am certain that there must have been a large proportion of Malay blood in his veins, for, unlike the Indians (from whom he differed also in complexion), he was extremely alert, active, nervous, and sensitive. A redeeming circumstance was his love for his master. Once his violent temper led him to the commission of an atrocious crime – the fatal stabbing of a dwarf. In punishment for this the rajah ordered that Neranya's right arm (the offending one) be severed from his body. The sentence was executed in a bungling fashion by a stupid fellow armed with an axe, and I, being a surgeon, was compelled, in order to save Neranya's life, to perform an amputation of the stump, leaving not a vestige of the limb remaining.

After this he developed an augmented fiendishness. His love for the rajah was changed to hate, and in his mad anger he flung discretion to the winds. Driven once to frenzy by the rajah's scornful treatment, he sprang upon the rajah with a knife but, fortunately, was seized and disarmed. To his unspeakable dismay the rajah sentenced him for this offence to suffer amputation of the remaining arm. It was done as in the former instance. This had the effect of putting a temporary curb on Neranya's spirit, or, rather, of changing the outward manifestations of his diabolism. Being armless, he was at first largely at the mercy of those who ministered to his needs – a duty which I undertook to see was properly discharged, for I felt an interest in this strangely distorted nature. His sense of helplessness, combined with a damnable scheme for revenge which he had secretly formed, caused Neranya to change his fierce, impetuous, and unruly conduct into a smooth, quiet, insinuating bearing, which he carried so artfully as to deceive those with whom he was brought in contact, including the rajah himself.

Neranya, being exceedingly quick, intelligent, and dexterous, and having an unconquerable will, turned his attention to the cultivating of an enlarged usefulness of his legs, feet, and toes, with so excellent effect that in time he was able to perform wonderful feats with those members.

Thus his capability, especially for destructive mischief, was considerably restored.

One morning the rajah's only son, a young man of an uncommonly amiable and noble disposition, was found dead in bed. His murder was a most atrocious one, his body being mutilated in a shocking manner, but in my eyes the most significant of all the mutilations was the entire removal and disappearance of the young prince's arms.

The death of the young man nearly brought the rajah to the grave. It was not, therefore, until I had nursed him back to health that I began a systematic inquiry into the murder. I said nothing of my own discoveries and conclusions until after the rajah and his officers had failed and my work had been done; then I submitted to him a written report, making a close analysis of all the circumstances, and closing by charging the crime to Neranya. The rajah, convinced by my proof and argument, at once ordered Neranya to be put to death, this to be accomplished slowly and with frightful tortures. The sentence was so cruel and revolting that it filled me with horror, and I implored that the wretch be shot. Finally, through a sense of gratitude to me, the rajah relaxed.

When Neranya was charged with the crime he denied it, of course, but, seeing that the rajah was convinced, he threw aside all restraint, and, dancing, laughing, and shrieking in the most horrible manner, confessed his guilt, gloated over it, and reviled the rajah to his teeth – this, knowing that some fearful death awaited him.

The rajah decided upon the details of the matter that night, and in the morning he informed me of his decision. It was that Neranya's life should be spared, but that both of his legs should be broken with hammers, and that then I should amputate the limbs at the trunk! Appended to this horrible sentence was a provision that the maimed wretch should be kept and tortured at regular intervals by such means as afterward might be devised.

Sickened to the heart by the awful duty set out for me, I nevertheless performed it with success, and I care to say nothing more about that part of the tragedy. Neranya escaped death very narrowly and was a long time in recovering his wonted vitality. During all these weeks the rajah neither saw him nor made inquiries concerning him, but when, as in duty bound, I made official report that the man had recovered his strength, the rajah's eyes brightened, and he emerged with deadly activity from the stupor into which he so long had been plunged.

The rajah's palace was a noble structure, but it is necessary here to describe only the grand hall. It was an immense chamber, with a floor of polished, inlaid stone and a lofty, arched ceiling. A soft light stole into it through stained glass set in the roof and in high windows on one side. In the middle of the room was a rich fountain, which threw up a tall, slender column of water, with smaller and shorter jets grouped around it. Across one end of the hail, halfway to the ceiling, was a balcony, which communicated with the upper story of a wing, and from which a flight of stone stairs descended to the floor of the hall. During the hot summers this room was delightfully cool; it was the rajah's favorite lounging place, and when the nights were hot he had his cot taken thither, and there he slept.

This hall was chosen for Neranya's permanent prison; here was he to stay so long as he might live, with never a glimpse of the shining world or the glorious heavens. To one of his nervous, discontented nature such confinement was worse than death. At the rajah's order there was constructed for him a small pen of open ironwork, circular, and about four feet in diameter, elevated on four slender iron posts, ten feet above the floor, and placed between the balcony and the fountain. Such was Neranya's prison. The pen was about four feet in depth, and the pen top was left open for the convenience of the servants whose duty it should be to care for him. These precautions for his safe confinement were taken at my suggestion, for, although the man was now deprived of all four of his limbs, I still feared that he might develop some extraordinary, unheard – of power for mischief. It was provided that the attendants should reach his cage by means of a movable ladder.

All these arrangements having been made, and Neranya hoisted into his cage, the rajah emerged upon the balcony to see him for the first time since the last amputation. Neranya had been lying panting and helpless on the floor of his cage, but when his quick ear caught the sound of the rajah's footfall he squirmed about until he had brought the back of his head against the railing, elevating his eyes above his chest, and enabling him to peer through the openwork of the cage. Thus the two deadly enemies faced each other. The rajah's stern face paled at sight of the hideous, shapeless thing which met his gaze; but he soon recovered, and the old hard, cruel, sinister look returned. Neranya's black hair and beard had grown long, and they added to the natural ferocity of his aspect. His eyes blazed upon the rajah with a terrible light, his lips parted, and he gasped for breath; his face was ashen with rage and despair, and his thin, distended nostrils quivered.

The rajah folded his arms and gazed down from the balcony upon the frightful wreck that he had made. Oh, the dreadful pathos of that picture; the inhumanity of it; the deep and dismal tragedy of it! Who might look into the wild, despairing heart of the prisoner and see and understand the frightful turmoil there; the surging, choking passion; unbridled but impotent ferocity; frantic thirst for a vengeance that should be deeper than hell! Neranya gazed, his shapeless body heaving, his eyes aflame; and then, in a strong, clear voice, which rang throughout the great hail, with rapid speech he hurled at the rajah the most insulting defiance, the most awful curses. He cursed the womb that had conceived him, the food that should nourish him, the wealth that had brought him power; cursed him in the name of Buddha and all the wise men; cursed by the sun, the moon, and the stars; by the continents, mountains, oceans, and rivers; by all things living; cursed his head, his heart, his entrails; cursed in a whirlwind of unmentionable words; heaped unimaginable insults and contumely upon him; called him a knave, a beast, a fool, a liar, an infamous and unspeakable coward.

The rajah heard it all calmly, without the movement of a muscle, without the slightest change of countenance; and when the poor wretch had exhausted his strength and fallen helpless and silent to the floor, the rajah, with a grim, cold smile, turned and strode away.

The days passed. The rajah, not deterred by Neranya's curses often heaped upon him, spent even more time than formerly in the great hall, and slept there oftener at night; and finally Neranya wearied of cursing and defying him, and fell into a sullen silence. The man was a study for me, and I observed every change in his fleeting moods. Generally his condition was that of miserable despair, which he attempted bravely to conceal. Even the boon of suicide had been denied him, for when he would wriggle into an erect position the rail of his pen was a foot above his head, so that he could not clamber over and break his skull on the stone floor beneath; and when he had tried to starve himself the attendants forced food down his throat; so that he abandoned such attempts. At times his eyes would blaze and his breath would come in gasps, for imaginary vengeance was working within him; but steadily he became quieter and more tractable, and was pleasant and responsive when I would converse with him. Whatever might have been the tortures which the rajah had decided on, none as yet had been ordered; and although Neranya knew that they were in contemplation, he never referred to them or complained of his lot.

The awful climax of this situation was reached one night, and even after this lapse of years I cannot approach its description without a shudder.

It was a hot night, and the rajah had gone to sleep in the great hall, lying on a high cot placed on the main floor just underneath the edge of the balcony. I had been unable to sleep in my own apartment, and so I had stolen into the great hall through the heavily curtained entrance at the end farthest from the balcony. As I entered I heard a peculiar, soft sound above the patter of the fountain. Neranya's cage was partly concealed from my view by the spraying water, but I suspected that the unusual sound came from him. Stealing a little to one side, and crouching against the dark hangings of the wall, I could see him in the faint light which dimly illuminated the hail, and then I discovered that my surmise was correct – Neranya was quietly at work.

Curious to learn more, and knowing that only mischief could have been inspiring him, I sank into a thick robe on the floor and watched him.

To my great astonishment Neranya was tearing off with his teeth the bag which served as his outer garment. He did it cautiously, casting sharp glances frequently at the rajah, who, sleeping soundly on his cot below, breathed heavily. After starting a strip with his teeth, Neranya, by the same means, would attach it to the railing of his cage and then wriggle away, much after the manner of a caterpillar's crawling, and this would cause the strip to be torn out the full length of his garment. He repeated this operation with incredible patience and skill until his entire garment had been torn into strips. Two or three of these he tied end to end with his teeth, lips, and tongue, tightening the knots by placing one end of the strip under his body and drawing the other taut with his teeth. In this way he made a line several feet long, one end of which he made fast to the rail with his mouth. It then began to dawn upon me that he was going to make an insane attempt – impossible of achievement without hands, feet, arms, or legs – to escape from his cage!

For what purpose? The rajah was asleep in the hall – ah! I caught my breath. Oh, the desperate, insane thirst for revenge which could have unhinged so clear and firm a mind! Even though he should accomplish the impossible feat of climbing over the railing of his cage that he might fall to the floor below (for how could he slide down the rope?), he would be in all probability killed or stunned; and even if he should escape these dangers, it would be impossible for him to clamber upon the cot without rousing the rajah, and impossible even though the rajah were dead!

Amazed at the man's daring, and convinced that his sufferings and brooding had destroyed his reason, nevertheless I watched him with breathless interest.

With other strips tied together he made a short swing across one side of his cage. He caught the long line in his teeth at a point not far from the rail; then, wriggling with great effort to an upright position, his back braced against the rail, he put his chin over the swing and worked toward one end. He tightened the grasp of his chin on the swing, and with tremendous exertion, working the lower end of his spine against the railing, he began gradually to ascend the side of his cage. The labor was so great that he was compelled to pause at intervals, and his breathing was hard and painful; and even while thus resting he was in a position of terrible strain, and his pushing against the swing caused it to press hard against his windpipe and nearly strangle him.

After amazing effort he had elevated the lower end of his body until it protruded above the railing, the top of which was now across the lower end of his abdomen. Gradually he worked his body over, going backward, until there was sufficient excess of weight on the outer side of the rail; and then, with a quick lurch, he raised his head and shoulders and swung into a horizontal position on top of the rail. Of course, he would have fallen to the floor below had it not been for the line which he held in his teeth. With so great nicety had he estimated the distance between his mouth and the point where the rope was fastened to the rail, that the line tightened and checked him just as he reached the horizontal position on the rail. If one had told me beforehand that such a feat as I had just seen this man accomplish was possible, I should have thought him a fool.

Neranya was now balanced on his stomach across the top of the rail, and he eased his position by bending his spine and hanging down on either side as much as possible. Having rested thus for some minutes, he began cautiously to slide off backward, slowly paying out the line through his teeth, finding almost a fatal difficulty in passing the knots. Now, it is quite possible that the line would have escaped altogether from his teeth laterally when he would slightly relax his hold to let it slip, had it not been for a very ingenious plan to which he had resorted. This consisted in his having made a turn of the line around his neck before he attacked the wing, thus securing a threefold control of the line – one by his teeth, another by friction against his neck, and a third by his ability to compress it between his cheek and shoulder. It was quite evident now that the minutest details of a most elaborate plan had been carefully worked out by him before beginning the task, and that possibly weeks of difficult theoretical study had been consumed in the mental preparation. As I observed him I was reminded of certain hitherto unaccountable things which he had been doing for some weeks past – going through certain hitherto inexplicable motions, undoubtedly for the purpose of training his muscles for the immeasurably arduous labor which he was now performing.

A stupendous and seemingly impossible part of his task had been accomplished. Could he reach the floor in safety? Gradually he worked himself backward over the rail, in imminent danger of falling; but his nerve never wavered, and I could see a wonderful light in his eyes.

With something of a lurch, his body fell against the outer side of the railing, to which he was hanging by his chin, the line still held firmly in his teeth. Slowly he slipped his chin from the rail, and then hung suspended by the line in his teeth. By almost imperceptible degrees, with infinite caution, he descended the line, and, finally, his unwieldy body rolled upon the floor, safe and unhurt!

What miracle would this superhuman monster next accomplish? I was quick and strong, and was ready and able to intercept any dangerous act; but not until danger appeared would I interfere with this extraordinary scene.

I must confess to astonishment upon having observed that Neranya, instead of proceeding directly toward the sleeping rajah, took quite another direction. Then it was only escape, after all, that the wretch contemplated, and not the murder of the rajah. But how could he escape? The only possible way to reach the outer air without great risk was by ascending the stairs to the balcony and leaving by the corridor which opened upon it, and thus fall into the hands of some British soldiers quartered thereabout, who might conceive the idea of hiding him; but surely it was impossible for Neranya to ascend that long flight of stairs! Nevertheless, he made directly for them, his method of progression this: He lay upon his back, with the lower end of his body toward the stairs; then bowed his spine upward, thus drawing his head and shoulders a little forward; straightened, and then pushed the lower end of his body forward a space equal to that through which he had drawn his head; repeating this again and again, each time, while bending his spine, preventing his head from slipping by pressing it against the floor. His progress was laborious and slow, but sensible; and, finally, he arrived at the foot of the stairs.

It was manifest that his insane purpose was to ascend them. The desire for freedom must have been strong within him! Wriggling to an upright position against the newel – post, he looked up at the great height which he had to climb, and sighed; but there was no dimming of the light in his eyes. How could he accomplish the impossible task?

His solution of the problem was very simple, though daring and perilous as all the rest. While leaning against the newel – post he let himself fall diagonally upon the bottom step, where he lay partly hanging over, but safe, on his side. Turning upon his back, he wriggled forward along the step to the rail and raised himself to an upright position against it as he had against the newel – post, fell as before, and landed on the second step. In this manner, with inconceivable labor, he accomplished the ascent of the entire flight of stairs.

It being apparent to me that the rajah was not the object of Neranya's movements, the anxiety which I had felt on that account was now entirely dissipated. The things which already he had accomplished were entirely beyond the nimblest imagination. The sympathy which I had always felt for the wretched man was now greatly quickened; and as infinitesimally small as I knew his chances for escape to be, I nevertheless hoped that he would succeed. Any assistance from me, however, was out of the question and it never should be known that I had witnessed the escape.

Neranya was now upon the balcony, and I could dimly see him wriggling along toward the door which led out upon the balcony.

Finally he stopped and wriggled to an upright position against the rail, which had wide openings between the balusters. His back was toward me, but he slowly turned and faced me and the hall. At that great distance I could not distinguish his features, but the slowness with which he had worked, even before he had fully accomplished the ascent of the stairs, was evidence all too eloquent of his extreme exhaustion. Nothing but a most desperate resolution could have sustained him thus far, but he had drawn upon the last remnant of his strength. He looked around the hall with a sweeping glance, and then down upon the rajah, who was sleeping immediately beneath him, over twenty feet below. He looked long and earnestly, sinking lower, and lower, and lower upon the rail. Suddenly, to my inconceivable astonishment and dismay, he toppled through and shot downward from his lofty height! I held my breath, expecting to see him crushed upon the stone floor beneath; but instead of that he fell full upon the rajah's breast, driving him through the cot to the floor. I sprang forward with a loud cry for help, and was instantly at the scene of the catastrophe. With indescribable horror I saw that Neranya's teeth were buried in the rajah's throat I tore the wretch away, but the blood was pouring from the rajah's arteries, his chest was crushed in, and he was gasping in the agony of death. People came running in, terrified. I turned to Neranya. He lay upon his back, his face hideously smeared with blood. Murder, and not escape, had been his intention from the beginning; and he had employed the only method by which there was ever a possibility of accomplishing it. I knelt beside him, and saw that he, too, was dying; his back had been broken by the fall. He smiled sweetly into my face, and a triumphant look of accomplished revenge sat upon his face even in death.

The Permanent Stiletto

I had sent in all haste for Dr. Rowell, but as yet he had not arrived, and the strain was terrible.

There lay my young friend upon his bed in the hotel, and I believe that he was dying. Only the jeweled handle of the knife was visible at his breast; the blade was wholly sheathed in his body.

"Pull it out, old fellow," begged the sufferer through white, drawn lips, his gasping voice being hardly less distressing than the unearthly look in his eyes.

"No, Arnold," said I, as I held his hand and gently stroked his forehead. It may have been instinct, it may have been a certain knowledge of anatomy that made me refuse.

"Why not? It hurts," he gasped. It was pitiful to see him suffer, this strong, healthy, daring, reckless young fellow.

Dr. Rowell walked in – a tall, grave man, with gray hair. He went to the bed and I pointed to the knife-handle, with its great, bold ruby in the end and its diamonds and emeralds alternating in quaint designs in the sides. The physician started. He felt Arnold pulse and looked puzzled.

"When was this done?" he asked.

"About twenty minutes ago," I answered.

The physician started out, beckoning me to follow.

"Stop!" said Arnold. We obeyed. "Do you wish to speak of me?" he asked.

"Yes," replied the physician, hesitating.

"Speak in my presence then," said my friend; "I fear nothing." It was in his old, imperious way, although his suffering must have been great.

"If you insist – " "I do."

"Then," said the physician, "if you have any matters to adjust they should be attended to at once. I can do nothing for you."

"How long can I live?" asked Arnold.

The physician thoughtfully stroked his gray beard. "It depends," he finally said; "if the knife be withdrawn you may live three minutes; if it be allowed o remain you may possibly live an hour or two – not longer."

Arnold never flinched.

"Thank you." he said, smiling faintly through his pain; "my friend here will pay you. I have some things to do. Let the knife remain." He turned his eves to mine, and, pressing my hand, said, affectionately, "And I thank you, too, old fellow, for not pulling it out."

The physician, moved by a sense of delicacy, left the room, saying, "Ring if there is a change. I will be in the hotel office." He had not gone far when he turned and came back. "Pardon me," he said, "but there is a young surgeon in this hotel who is said to be a very skillful man. My specialty is not surgery, but medicine. May I call him?"

"Yes," said I, eagerly; but Arnold smiled and shook his head. "I fear there will not be time," he said. But I refused to heed him and directed the surgeon to be called immediately. I was writing at Arnold's dictation when the two men entered the room.

There was something of nerve and assurance in the young surgeon that struck my attention. His manner, though quiet, was bold and straightforward and his movements sure and quick. This young man had already distinguished himself in the performance of some difficult hospital laparotomies, and he was at that sanguine age when ambition looks through the spectacles of experiment. Dr. Raoul Entrefort was the new-corner's name. He was a Creole, small and dark, and he had travelled and studied in Europe.

"Speak freely," gasped Arnold, after Dr. Entrefort had made an examination.

"What think you, doctor?" asked Entrefort of the older man.

"I think," was the reply, "that the knife-blade has penetrated the ascending aorta, about two inches above the heart. So long as the blade remains in the wound, the escape of blood is comparatively small, though certain; were the blade withdrawn the heart would almost instantly empty itself through the aortal wound."

Meanwhile, Entrefort was deftly cutting away the white shirt and the undershirt, and soon had the breast exposed. He examined the gem-studded hilt with keenest interest.

"You are proceeding on the assumption, doctor," he said, "that this weapon is a knife."

"Certainly," answered Dr. Rowell, smiling; "what else can it be?"

"It is a knife," faintly interposed Arnold.

"Did you see the blade?" Entrefort asked him, quickly.

"I did – for a moment."

Entrefort shot a quick look at Dr. Rowell and whispered, "Then it is not suicide." Dr. Rowell looked puzzled and said nothing.

"I must disagree with you, gentlemen," quietly remarked Entrefort; "this is not a knife." He examined the handle very narrowly. Not only was the blade entirely concealed from view within Arnold's body, but the blow had been so strongly delivered that the skin was depressed by the guard. "The fact that it is not a knife presents a very curious series of facts and contingencies. "

pursued Entrefort, with amazing coolness, "some of which are, so far as I am informed, entirely novel in the history of surgery."

A quizzical expression, faintly amused and manifestly interested, was upon Dr. Rowell's face.

"What is the weapon, doctor?" he asked.

"A stiletto."

Arnold started. Dr. Rowell appeared confused. "I must confess," he said, "my ignorance of the differences among these penetrating weapons, whether dirks, daggers, stilettos, poniards, or bowie-knives."

"With the exception of the stiletto," explained Entrefort, "all the weapons you mention have one or two edges, so that in penetrating they cut their way. A stiletto is round, is ordinarily about half an inch or less in diameter at the guard, and tapers to a sharp point. It penetrates solely by pushing the tissue aside in all directions. You will understand the importance of that point."

Dr. Rowell nodded, more deeply interested than ever.

"How do you know it is a stiletto, Dr. Entrefort?" I asked.

"The cutting of these stones is the work of Italian lapidaries," he said, "and they were set in Genoa. Notice, too, the guard. It is much broader and shorter than the guard of an edged weapon; in fact, it is nearly round. The weapon is about four hundred years old, and would be cheap at twenty thousand florins. Observe, also, the darkening color of your friend's breast in the immediate vicinity of the guard; this indicates that the tissues have been bruised by the crowding of the 'blade,' if I may use the term."

"What has all of this to do with me?" asked the dying man.

"Perhaps a great deal, perhaps nothing. It brings a single ray of hope into your desperate condition." Arnold's eyes sparkled and he caught his breath. A tremor passed all through him, and I felt it in the hand I was holding. Life was sweet to him, then, after all, sweet to this wild dare-devil who had just faced death with such calmness! Dr. Rowell, though showing no sign of jealousy, could not conceal a look of incredulity.

"With your permission," said Entrefort, addressing Arnold, "I will do what I can to save your life."

"You may," said the poor boy.

"But I shall have to hurt you."

"Well."

"Perhaps very much."

"Well."

"And even if I succeed (the chance is one in a thousand) you will never be a sound man, and a constant and terrible danger will always be present."

"Well."

Entrefort wrote a note and sent it away in haste by a bell-boy.

"Meanwhile," he resumed, "your life is in imminent danger from shock, and the end may come in a few minutes or hours from that cause. Attend without delay to whatever matters may require settling, and Dr. Rowell," glancing at that gentleman, "will give you something to brace you up. I speak frankly, for I see that you are a man of extraordinary nerve. Am I right?"

"Be perfectly candid," said Arnold.

Dr. Rowell, evidently bewildered by his cyclonic young associate, wrote a prescription, which I sent by a boy to be filled. With unwise zeal I asked Entrefort, "Is there not danger of lockjaw?"

"No," he replied; "there is not a sufficiently extensive injury to peripheral nerves to induce traumatic tetanus."

I subsided. Dr. Rowell's medicine came and I administered a dose. The physician and the surgeon then retired. The poor sufferer straightened up his business. When it was done he asked me, "What is that crazy Frenchman going to do to me?"

"I have no idea, be patient."

In less than an hour before they returned, bringing with them a keen-eyed, tall young man, who had a number of tools wrapped in an apron. Evidently he was unused to such scenes, for he became deathly pale upon seeing the ghastly spectacle on my bed. With staring eyes and open mouth he began to retreat towards the door, stammering, – "I – I can't do it."

"Nonsense, Hippolyte! Don't be a baby. Why, man, it is a case of life and death!"

"But – look at his eyes! he is dying!"

Arnold smiled. "I am not dead, though," he gasped.

"I – I beg your pardon," said Hippolyte.

Dr. Entrefort gave the nervous man a drink of brandy and then said, "No more nonsense, my boy; it must be done. Gentlemen, allow me to introduce Mr. Hippolyte, one of the most original, ingenious, and skillful machinists in the country."

Hippolyte, being modest, blushed as he bowed. In order to conceal his confusion he unrolled his apron on the table with considerable noise of rattling tools.

"I have to make some preparations before you may begin, Hippolyte, and I want you to observe me that you may become used for only to the sight of fresh blood, but also, what is more trying, the odor of it."

Hippolyte shivered. Entrefort opened a case of surgical instruments. "Now, doctor, the chloroform," he said, to Dr. Rowell.

"I will not take it," promptly interposed the sufferer; "I want to know when I die."

"Very well," said Entrefort; "but you have little nerve now to spare. We may try it without chloroform, however. It will be better if you can do without. Try your best to lie still while I cut."

"What are you going to do?" asked Arnold.

"Save your life, if possible."

"How? Tell me about it."

"Must you know?"

"Yes."

"Very well, then. The point of the stiletto has passed entirely through the aorta, which is the great vessel rising out of the heart and carrying the aerated blood to the arteries. If I should withdraw the weapon the blood would rush from the two holes in the aorta and you would soon be dead. If the weapon had been a knife, the parted tissue would have yielded, and the blood would have been forced out on either side of the blade and would have caused death. As it is, not a drop of blood has escaped from the aorta into the thoracic cavity. All that is left for us to do, then, is to allow the stiletto to remain permanently in the aorta. Many difficulties at once present themselves, and I do not wonder at Dr. Rowell's look of surprise and incredulity."

That gentleman smiled and shook his head.

"It is a desperate chance," continued Entrefort, "and is a novel case in surgery; but it is the only chance. The fact that the weapon is a stiletto is the important point – a stupid weapon, but a blessing to us now. If the assassin had known more she would have used–"

Upon his employment of the noun "assassin" and the feminine pronoun "she," both Arnold and I started violently, and I cried out to the man to stop.

"Let him proceed," said Arnold, who, by a remarkable effort, had calmed himself.

"Not if the subject is painful," Entrefort said.

"It is not," protested Arnold; "why do you think the blow was struck by a woman?"

"Because, first, no man capable of being an assassin would use so gaudy and valuable a weapon; second, no man would be so stupid as to carry so antiquated and inadequate a thing as a stiletto, when that most murderous and satisfactory of all penetrating and cutting weapons, the bowie-knife, is available. She was a strong woman, too, for it requires a good hand to drive a stiletto to the guard, even though it misses the sternum by a hairs breadth and slip between the ribs, for the muscles here are hard and the intercostal spaces narrow. She was not only a strong woman, but a desperate one also."

"That will do," said Arnold. He beckoned me to bend closer. "You must watch this man; he is too sharp; he is dangerous."

"Then," resumed Entrefort, "I shall tell you what I intend to do. There will undoubtedly be inflammation of the aorta, which, if it persist, will cause a fatal aneurysm by a breaking down of the aortal walls; but we hope, with the help of your youth and health, to check it.

"Another serious difficulty is this: With every inhalation, the entire thorax (or bony structure of the chest) considerably expands. The aorta remains stationary. You will see, therefore, that as your aorta and breast are now held in rigid relation to each other by the stiletto, the chest, with every inhalation, pulls the aorta forward out of place about half an inch. I am certain that it is doing this, because there is no indication of an escape of arterial blood into the thoracic cavity; in other words, the mouths of the two aortal wounds have seized upon the blade with a firm hold and thus prevent it from slipping in and out. This is a very fortunate occurrence, but one which will cause pain for some time. The aorta, you may understand, being made by the stiletto to move with the breathing, pulls the heart backward and forward with every breath you take; but that organ, though now undoubtedly much surprised, will accustom itself to its new condition.

"What I fear most, however, is the formation of a clot around the blade. You see, the presence of the blade in the aorta has already reduced the blood-carrying capacity of that vessel; a clot, therefore, need not be very large to stop up the aorta, and, of course, if that should occur death would ensue. But the clot, if one form, may be dislodged and driven forward, in which event it may lodge in any one of the numerous branches from the aorta and produce results more or less serious, possibly fatal. If, for instance, it should choke either the right or the left carotid, there would ensue atrophy of one side of the brain, and consequently paralysis of half the entire body; but it is possible that in time there would come about a secondary circulation from the other side of the brain, and thus restore a healthy condition. Or the clot (which, in passing always from larger arteries to smaller, must unavoidably find one not sufficiently large to carry it, and must lodge somewhere) may either necessitate amputation of one of the four limbs or lodge itself so deep within the body that it cannot be reached with the knife. You are beginning to realize some of the dangers which await you."

Arnold smiled faintly.

"But we shall do our best to prevent the formation of a clot," continued Entrefort; "there are drugs which may be used with effect."

"Are there more dangers?"

"Many more; some of the more serious have not been mentioned. One of these is the probability of the aortal tissues pressing upon the weapon relaxing their hold and allowing the blade to slip. That would let out the blood and cause death. I am uncertain whether the hold is now maintained by the pressure of the tissues or the adhesive quality of the serum which was set free by the puncture. I am convinced, though, that in either event the hold is easily broken and that it may give way at any moment, for it is under several kinds of strains. Every time the heart contracts and crowds the blood into the aorta, the latter expands a little, and then contracts when the pressure is removed. Any unusual exercise or excitement produces stronger and quicker hearts-beats, and increases the strain on the adhesion of the aorta to the weapon. A fright, a fall, a jump, a blow on the chest, any of these might so jar the heart and aorta as to break the hold."

Entrefort stopped.

"Is that all?" asked Arnold.

"No; but is not that enough?"

"More than enough," said Arnold, with a sudden and dangerous sparkle in his eyes. Before any of us could think, the desperate fellow had seized the handle of the stiletto with both hands in a determined effort to withdraw it and die. I had had no time to order my faculties to the movement of a muscle, when Entrefort, with incredible alertness and swiftness, had Arnold's wrists. Slowly Arnold relaxed his hold.

"There, now!" said Entrefort, soothingly; "that was a careless act and might have broken the adhesion! You'll have to be careful."

Arnold look at him with a curious combination of expressions.

"Dr. Entrefort," he quietly remarked, "you are the devil."

Bowing profoundly, Entrefort replied: "You do me too great an honor;" then he whispered to his patient: "If you do that" – with a motion towards the hilt – "I will have her hanged for murder." Arnold started and choked, and a look of horror overspread his face. He withdrew his hands, took one of mine in both of his, threw his arms upon the pillow above his head, and, holding my hand, firmly said to Entrefort, "Proceed with your work."

"Come closer, Hippolyte," said Entrefort, "and observe narrowly. Will you kindly assist me, Dr. Rowell?" That gentleman had sat in wondering silence.

Entrefort's hand was quick and sure, and he used the knife with marvelous dexterity. First he made four equidistant incisions outward from the guard and just through the skin. Arnold held his breath and ground his teeth at the first cut, but soon regained command of himself. Each incision was about two inches long. Hippolyte shuddered and turned his head aside. Entrefort, whom nothing escaped. exclaimed, "Steady, Hippolyte! Observe!"

Quickly was the skin peeled back to the limit of the incisions. This must have been excruciatingly painful. Arnold groaned, and his hands were moist and cold. Down sank the knife into the flesh from which the skin had been raised, and blood flowed freely; Dr. Rowell handled the sponge. The keen knife worked rapidly. Arnold's marvelous nerve was breaking down. He clutched my hand fiercely; his eyes danced; his mind was weakening. Almost in a moment the flesh had been cut away to the bones, which were now exposed, two ribs and the sternum. A few quick cuts cleared the weapon between the guard and the ribs.

"To work, Hippolyte – be quick!"

The machinist had evidently been coached before he came. With slender, long-fingered hands, which trembled at first, he selected certain tools with nice precision, made some rapid measurements of the weapon and of the cleared space around it, and began to adjust the pans of a queer little machine. Arnold watched him curiously.

"What– " he began to say; but he ceased; a deeper pallor set on his face, his hands relaxed, and his eyelids fell.

"Thank God!" exclaimed Entrefort; "he has fainted – he can't stop us now. Quick, Hippolyte!"

The machinist attached the queer little machine to the handle of the weapon, seized the stiletto in his left hand, and with his right began a series of sharp, rapid movements backward and forward.

"Hurry, Hippolyte!" urged Entrefort.

"The metal is very hard."

"Is it cutting?"

"I can't see for the blood."

In another moment something snapped. Hippolyte started; he was very nervous. He removed the little machine.

"The metal is very hard." he said; "it breaks the saws."

He adjusted another tiny saw and resumed work. After a little while he picked up the handle of the stiletto and laid it on the table. He had cut it off, leaving the blade inside Arnold's body.

"Good, Hippolyte!" exclaimed Entrefort. In a minute he had closed the bright end of the blade from view by drawing together the skin-flaps and sewing them firmly.

Arnold returned to consciousness and glanced down at his breast. He seemed puzzled. "Where is the weapon?" he asked.

"Here is part of it," answered Entrefort, holding up the handle.

"And the blade – " "That is an irremovable part of your internal machinery." Arnold was silent. "It had to be cut off," pursued Entrefort, "not only because it would be troublesome and an undesirable ornament, but also because it was advisable to remove every possibility of its withdrawal." Arnold said nothing. "Here is a prescription," said Entrefort; "take the medicine as directed for the next five years without fail."

"What for? I see that it contains muriatic acid."

"If necessary I will explain five years from now."

"If I live."

"If you live."

Arnold drew me down to him and whispered, "Tell her to fly at once; this man may make trouble for her."

Was there ever a more generous fellow?

◆ ◆ ◆ ◆ ◆

I thought that I recognized a thin, pale, bright face among the passengers who were leaving an Australian steamer which had just arrived at San Francisco.

"Dr. Entrefort!" I cried.

"Ah!" he said, peering up mm my face and grasping my hand; "I know you now, but you have changed. You remember that I was called away immediately after I had performed that crazy operation on your friend. I have spent the intervening four years in India, China, Tibet, Siberia, the South Seas, and God knows where not. But wasn't that a most absurd, hare-brained experiment that I tried on your friend! Still, it was all that could have been done. I have dropped all that nonsense long ago. It is better, for more reasons than one, to let them die at once. Poor fellow! he bore it so bravely! Did he suffer much after-wards? How long did he live? A week perhaps a month?"

"He is alive yet."

"What!" exclaimed Entrefort, startled.

"He is, indeed, and is in this city."

"Incredible!"

"It is true; you shall see him."

"But tell me about him now!" cried the surgeon, his eager eyes glittering with the peculiar light which I had seen in them on the night of the operation. "Has he regularly taken the medicine which I pre-scribed?"

"He has. Well, the change in him, from what he was before the operation, is shocking. Imagine a young dare-devil of twenty-two, who had no greater fear of danger or death than of a cold, now a cringing, cowering fellow; apparently an old man, nursing his life with pitiful tenderness, fearful that at any moment something may happen to break the hold of his aorta walls on the stiletto-blade; a confirmed hypo-chondriac, peevish, melancholic, unhappy in the extreme. He keeps himself confined as closely as possible, avoiding all excitement and exercise, and even reads nothing exciting. The constant danger has worn out the last shred of his manhood and left him a pitiful wreck. Can nothing be done for him?"

"Possibly. But has he consulted no physician?"

"None whatever; he has been afraid that he might learn the worst."

"Let us find him at once. Ah, here comes my wife to meet me! She arrived by the other steamer." I recognized her immediately and was overcome with astonishment.

"Charming woman," said Entrefort; "you'll like her. We were married three years ago at Bombay. She belongs to a noble Italian family and has travelled a great deal."

He introduced us. To my unspeakable relief she remembered neither my name nor my face. I must have appeared odd to her, but it was impossible for me to be perfectly unconcerned. We went to Arnold's rooms, I much with dread. I left her in the reception-room and took Entrefort within. Arnold was too greatly absorbed in his own troubles to be dangerously excited by meeting Entrefort, whom he greeted with indifferent hospitality.

"But I heard a woman's voice," he said. "It sounds–" He checked himself, and before I could intercept him he had gone to the reception-room; and there he stood face to face with the beautiful adventuress, – none other than Entrefort's wife now, – who, wickedly desperate, had driven a stiletto into Arnold's vitals in a hotel four years before because he had refused to marry her. They recognized each other instantly and both grew pale; but she, quicker witted, recovered her composure at once and advanced towards him with a smile and an extended hand. He stepped back, his face ghastly with fear.

"Oh!" he gasped, "the excitement, the shock, it has made the blade slip out! The blood is pouring from the opening, – it burns, – I am dying!" and he fell into my arms and instantly expired.

The autopsy revealed the surprising fact that there was no blade in his thorax at all; it had been gradually consumed by the muriatic acid which Entrefort had prescribed for that very purpose, and the perforations in the aorta had closed up gradually with the wasting of the blade and had been perfectly healed for a long time. All his vital organs were sound. My poor friend, once so reckless and brave, had died simply of a childish and groundless fear, and the woman unwittingly had accomplished her revenge.

The Haunted Automaton

Old man Erkins had three principal faults: he was rich, stingy, and a hard drinker. For the first of these he was to blame; for the second, pitied; for the third – but wait and read further before you express an opinion. At all events, by reason of these things and of others that I shall now write concerning him, I say and you will say that he should have been killed; which I am restrained from doing in this very line by the necessities of this story and not at all by fear either of the law or of punishment in the world to come.

Upon recovering from a hard spree, toward the end of which he would begin to see strange things, Erkins would not touch a drop for several days; then, recovering his nerve, he would laugh at his past timidity and – take a drink; the next day one, the next three, the next four, and so on, until snakes and other queer things would creep out of dark places.

There was an old servant, named Sarah, that kept his large prison (for such was his house) in order; and the one green spot in her shaky old life was a pretty girl, old Erkins' niece, ward and prisoner combined – Alice by name, and the prettiest girl in all the country thereabout, though a very unhappy one, to be sure. Alice had inherited Sarah, who was Alice's mother's trusted servant, and who vowed that she never, never would leave the poor young orphan, though the old house should swarm with snakes and things.

Now, the old miser loved his niece in a certain way. There are persons who love others so deeply that they murder them. There are various ways of committing murder, and one of the cruelest is to shut up a pretty girl in a big house and never let a young fellow even look at her.

Merely because she accidentally – entirely accidentally – fell in love with a poor but good-looking young machinist whom she met at church, her old guardian, in a spirit of mean tyranny, forbade her ever going out again, and in a most insulting and over-bearing manner told this young man, Howard Rankin, that the girl should never see him again, and that any mendicant fortune-hunter who should ever present himself at the house or seek to capture her for her quarter of a million would be riddled with buckshot.

Old Erkins had a mania for curious mechanisms. He had clocks that did all manner of wonderful things, and hundreds of other ingenious contrivances of various kinds. Whenever he read of some curious invention he would have it. He never tired of amusing himself with these things. There was one thing that Erkins needed to complete his happiness as well as his collection, and that was an automaton – a working counterfeit man. He had read everything that had ever been written on the subject of such automata. He had visited museums and wax-works shows, and had seen gladiators and Zouaves dying their several deaths again and again; but they were all too suggestive, for there were times when old Erkins' nerves were weak. Once he did buy a dying gladiator at enormous expense, but on the occasion of his next bad spell that gladiator's departing life seemed to take the form of numberless snakes and monkeys; and, frantic with fright, its owner chopped it to pieces with a hatchet.

Howard Rankin had a certain inventive genius. Knowing the old mans weakness, he conceived the idea of constructing an automaton, with which he hoped, he told a friend, to reinstate himself in the old man's good graces. However, this was a secret. All that he gave out was that he was going to construct an automaton – he knew what would result. He really did think that he loved Alice very, very deeply. Why shouldn't he? He promptly began to put his idea into execution, and selected the back room of his work-shop.

Very soon the project caused such talk that old Erkins heard of it. As the work progressed and favored bends were permitted to see the wonderful automaton as it grew under its author's hands, old Erkins, hearing the stories, became more and more interested. When a few months had passed he heard that the automaton was nearly finished.

Erkins could restrain himself no longer – he must see that automaton and must secure it. But how should he proceed? He had grossly insulted the inventor. This was a serious difficulty. He pondered over it a few days, and then boldly sent a polite note, asking permission to see the automaton. A formal note, granting the request, came in reply. The old man went at once.

The young man received him with polite condescension. Erkins' keen old eyes glittered eagerly; and Howard, noticing it, was secretly elated accordingly. Outwardly he was stiff and cold.

"And so you are at work on an automaton?" Erkins asked, as he was ushered into the back room.

"Yes," deliberately responded the young mechanic, as he quietly proceeded with his work.

"Cheerful one?"

"What?"

"Cheerful?"

"What do you mean?"

"It doesn't die, or anything of that sort, does it?"

"Oh, no!"

"'Cause I had a dying gladiator once, and it died so hard that sna— that – that it was unpleasant."

He stepped closer to the half finished automaton. It sat in an easy-chair. "So I killed it," he said.

"Killed what?"

"Gladiator."

He was devoured with curiosity concerning Howard's automaton, and yet felt such timidity that he hesitated about asking questions. Howard, volunteering no information, continued his work. Presently Erkins mustered up courage.

"I see you haven't put on its head yet," he essayed.

"No."

"Haven't got it ready?"

"No."

There was a pause.

"What will it do?"

"A good many things."

The old man went round it and examined it narrowly. It was the figure of a fop, dressed in the extreme of fashion, sitting in an indolent posture.

"Everything finished except the head, eh?"

"Yes," answered Howard; who seeing that he had carried his indifference far enough, left off his work, and said: "The head is to be the main part, because the more important work is to be done by it, and great care is required in making its wax face, its eyes, and so forth. Here is the block of it, with the machinery inside. That blonde wig will be its hair. As the automaton now is, however, it can give all the limb motions, though they are comparatively insignificant." Howard inserted a key in a hole in the back of the chair and wound up the automaton. The slight clicking of machinery was audible. Old Erkins trembled with excitement as he saw the automaton begin to move. It brought its right hand to the place where its mouth would be, then lowered it; brought up its left hand, and then crossed its legs.

"The right hand," explained Howard, "will carry a cigar, for the automaton will smoke. See – it will take a few puffs and then withdraw the cigar. The other hand is now taking up an eye-glass. I must now stop the machinery, as other attachments, not yet supplied, will have to be added, and still other machinery, the most intricate of all, is contained within the head."

"What will you do with the automaton?" asked Erkins, feeling his way.

"Don't know – probably keep it for my own amusement."

"Wouldn't you sell it?"

"Sell it! why, who is rich enough to buy it!"

Erkins' heart sank.

"What shall you ask for it?" he inquired in sheer desperation.

"A thousand dollars."

Erkins' heart leaped with joy.

"I'll take it," he eagerly said. He had expected to hear five-thousand. "It's a go," quietly responded Howard.

Then Erkins began to reflect that possibly he had been too hasty.

"I may be giving you too much," he said.

"Don't take it if you don't want it," coolly answered the young man.

"Will you give me a written guaranty of what it will do?" he asked.

Howard pondered a moment. "I will do not only that," he said, "but more; for I have great confidence in the automaton. Let me see. This is the 12th of November. I will be married on Wednesday, the 24th of next month, the day before Christmas. I shall want eight hundred dollars for my wedding and to start in life. I – "

"Married!" exclaimed old Erkins in astonishment.

"Yes. I will take eight hundred dollars down. If the automaton please you, you are to pay the balance; if in any particular it fall below your expectations, you may keep the two hundred. I will give you a written guaranty that the automaton shall cross and uncross its legs, smoke cigars, adjust its eye-glass, incline its head, open and close its eyes, wink and talk – speak two or three words."

"Good!" cried the old man. "It's a bargain." Erkins was very happy when he left. He had had two triumphs – secured the automaton and learned that Alice and her fortune were no longer in danger.

According to agreement the automaton was delivered on Saturday, December 20th, by a friend of Howard's, the inventor sending word that under the circumstances he had no desire to enter Mr. Erkins' house. The automaton was encased in a large box provided with handles, and four men were brought to carry it into the house. Old Erkins danced about in great excitement and high glee. It was a time of such rejoicing with him that he called Alice and Old Sarah to share his happiness and see the wonderful automaton. Much of his exhilaration was due to drink, for the old man was rapidly reaching the limit, and in two or three days his old wriggling friends would surely be upon him.

"How's Rankin getting along with his wedding?" asked Erkins of the friend.

The latter gave some offhand reply, and as he did so he saw Alice stagger backward to the wall and her face blanch. "By the way, Alice," said wicked old Erkins, delighting in the cruel stab he was giving, "Howard Rankin is to be married next Wednesday."

The poor girl could say nothing, for her heart was broken; but old Erkins did not notice her strange conduct nor see the agony of shame, humiliation and despair she suffered. Sarah saw it all, and it wrung her faithful old heart. She slipped her arm around the young girl's waist and would have led her away; but Erkins commanded them to remain, and Erkins' word was law.

The men set down the big box in the hall.

"Mr. Erkins," said the friend, "here are certain instructions that Howard sent for the management of the automaton. He insists that they be carried out to the letter, or he will not be responsible for failure."

The old man hastily read the instructions. Among them there was this one: "The automaton must be kept in a room with a temperature not below 65 degrees Fahrenheit nor above 75 degrees, otherwise the springs, catgut strings, the wax of the face and of the head, and the glue of the various parts will be ruined." Here was another: "There must be little light in the room, or the delicate colors in the face and hands will fade; and the automaton must not be placed with its face to the light" Another instruction made careful provision for ventilation, thus: "Exterior air, which at this time of year is either damp or frosty, must be excluded, and hence the window should never be opened; but as fresh air is necessary, the door must always be left slightly ajar – say six inches – and it must not open into any other room, but into a hall." Winding at night or more than once a day was forbidden. There were also minute instructions for preparing and lighting the cigars that the automaton should smoke.

Erkins reflected. There was only one room in the house which permitted of compliance with these instructions, and that was up-stairs. He slept down-stairs, and he had intended to place it in a room adjoining his bedroom; but as he used that one for an office and kept a hot fire in it, the automaton would be ruined there. The only objection he had to its going up-stairs was upon account of his fear that Sarah or Alice, who occupied rooms near the one that must receive the automaton, would surreptitiously wind up the treasure at unseasonable times and thus ruin it. But had he been shrewd enough to guess at the loathing they had for a thing that came from Howard's hands, he would have felt no uneasiness.

"Sarah," he sternly said, "I must put the automaton in the southwest room up-stairs; but if either you or Alice dare to touch it or enter the room where it is, I'll murder you. Do you understand that? I'll murder you both."

The four men carried the big box to the southwest room up-stairs and set it just where it should be, according to the instructions. Old Erkins, gleeful and brutal, forced Sarah and Alice to accompany it, and compelled them to stand and see it uncovered. This was done by removing the top, ends, and sides of the box and lifting a cloth that covered the figure. The wonderful automaton sat revealed.

Alice had secretly hoped that Howard had made the automaton to resemble himself, though ever so slightly; but when she saw the figure, with flaxen hair and mustache, so different from his, which were black; and the broad black eyebrows; and the painted cheeks, so different from his own pale face; and the foppish costume; and the effeminately curled hair; and the general air of impudence that pervaded the whole figure, her last hope departed. There was not a shadow of Howard's quiet manliness in anything about this mimic man.

Old Erkins regarded it otherwise. He saw only a wonderful mechanism, finished and decked out with fine art; and that was all he cared for. The artificial fop reclined indolently in an easy-.chair. Its head hung upon its breast and its eyes were closed, its appearance being that of a slumbering man.

The four carriers were dismissed, and the friend produced a key, inserted it in a hole in the back of the chair, and wound up the automaton. It raised its head, opened its eyes sleepily, and with the greatest dignity it slowly turned its head as though regarding each member of the company, and then it smiled and very graciously bowed. Howard's friend produced a cigar and carefully prepared it, as a lesson to Erkins, the automaton meanwhile continuing to bow and smile. Following the instructions, the friend laid the cigar on a little stand convenient to the automaton's right hand, and the automaton with absolutely accurate movement brought the cigar to its mouth and with great deliberation took several puffs. Then it removed the cigar, and with its left hand adjusted an eyeglass, with which it gravely regarded the company; then puffed at the cigar again, and then crossed its legs.

"I must go now," said the friend. "The automaton will keep this up thirty minutes longer, and then it will have run down; but it must not be wound again till to-morrow. Remember the instructions"; and he left.

Alice then begged to be allowed to go, as she was dying with a headache, she said, and had seen enough of the automaton; and so old Erkins, deeply disgusted, dismissed them.

He remained alone with the automaton, sitting directly in front of it and eagerly drinking with his eyes every one of the slow, dignified, accurate motions that it made. The only sound audible was a faint ticking, a very soft creaking, of the intricate machinery. This comparative silence, and the subtle wisdom that the automaton seemed to have and its deliberate manner, and its impudence, began to work upon Erkins' diseased imagination. As the thing continued to smoke, and adjust its eyeglass, and cross its legs, and open and close its eyes and bow so gravely, it took on, in Erkins' opinion, a kind of uncanny, supernatural air that disturbed its owner. Erkins' mind was not exactly right, and he knew it; but even making due allowance for it he was positive the thing was acting strangely. It seemed to be trying to exasperate him. This feeling was steadily growing upon Erkins; so that when there came a sharp little click in the machinery and the automaton dropped the cigar to the floor and boldly winked at Erkins, the old man began to experience downright fright. Yet he reflected that the guaranty called for winks. Still, this wink was too knowing. It was an insidious, wise, searching wink, that seemed to show cognizance of every sin that Erkins had ever committed. It was a leering, impudent wink; such a wink as innocence would be incapable of; a dangerous, mocking wink. It winked not only once, but twice, thrice, four times; taking a long time between winks, and accompanying each with a sinister leer. It did nothing but wink. Everything about it was perfectly still with the exception of that one eye-lid, and the stare that it kept fastened upon Erkins was a cold and deadly stare; a stare that saw through and through him, he thought, and that acted upon him with such strange effect that it held him bound, cold with terror, to his seat.

It was also in the guaranty that the automaton should speak. As yet it had not spoken. When it had winked several times there came another sharp little click, which startled Erkins. The old man had forgotten all about the speaking, but that little click warned him that something else was coming. What would it be? Something awful, he instinctively felt.

The automaton sat still for five long seconds, and then very slowly, very cautiously, very mysteriously, it leaned forward and said in a hollow, ghostly voice, that seemed to come up from the bowels of the earth:

"I'm haunted!" Erkins shivered, and he thought his heart had ceased beating. The automaton slowly resumed its former posture and fixed its dead stare upon its owner. It sat thus for what seemed to Erkins an age, and then again as before it leaned forward and in sepulchral tones it said:

"I'm haunted!"

Erkins could hear it no longer. White and trembling with fright, he backed out of the room, carefully left the door as the specifications required, and went out into the garden and shook himself like a dog.

"That thing," he muttered, "is worse than a sna— than the dying gladiator. But it's a beautiful piece of work," he presently added, when he had somewhat recovered his nerve; "and of course I shall get used to it. Of course."

Nevertheless, he needed something to help him in this and he sought it in his liquor. He drank frightfully all that day, and toward evening his old unwelcome visitors began to show themselves. And they were unusually bold. He went early to bed, and actually one hideous old monkey had the effrontery to pretend he was a dying gladiator.

A young monkey assumed all the airs of a fop, and smoked a cigar, adjusted an eye-glass, crossed its legs, smiled and bowed, and then winked at the miserable old man in the most impudent and insulting manner; and, not satisfied with that, it leaned forward mysteriously from its perch on the foot-board of the bed, and in a rasping, sepulchral whisper, said:

"I'm haunted!"

Thus passed this hideous night – one of snakes, monkeys, dying gladiators, fops who declared they were haunted, and horrible nightmares.

But Sunday morning came at last, and old Erkins ushered in the new day with deep draughts of brandy. He was trying to steady himself for a second interview with the automaton.

At last he entered the automaton's room. There sat the ingeniously constructed thing, sound asleep in its chair. Erkins approached it gingerly, but it sat so quiet and harmless, and looked so weak and effeminate, and so unlike the ghostly thing that leered and winked at him the day before, declaring it was haunted, that his courage revived and he laughed at his fright. The old fellow was badly shattered from drinking, and his old knees tottered and his bony hands trembled as he went to the mantel and returned with the key to wind the automaton. He was very nervous and jerky about the winding; but he managed to get through with it in a fashion, and then he sat down in front of the automaton and awaited developments. The same old motions were exactly repeated, although the automaton had to puff an imaginary cigar, as Erkins was too badly shaken up to remember it. But the oversight soon began to trouble him. In his befogged condition of mind he imagined that the automaton laid it up against him. He was positive that under the smile lurked a wicked look, and he was thoroughly convinced of this when the first click came and the winking and leering commenced. There was then exhibited by that soft-appearing automaton a diabolical deviltry and a deeply mysterious cunning that no mechanical thing – so Erkins thought – could show; and when it came to the second click, and began slowly to lean forward, the horrible thought stole into the old man's mind that the devil himself sat before him.

"I'm haunted!"

Erkins' blood ran cold. He suffered an agony of fright. Every nerve quivered, and he gasped for breath. A deathly perspiration exuded from his face and trickled down his cheeks. With hands upraised and fingers outspread, with gaping mouth and wide-staring eyes, he gazed with a terrible, tragic fascination at the awful thing before him.

"I'm haunted!" The blind yet ever-watchful instinct of self-preservation dragged the old man tottering from his seat and thrust him out. Stumbling, staggering, mumbling, he found his way to his own room, and fell headlong upon the floor, and passed into grateful unconsciousness.

He lay thus an hour or more, and recovering, crawled to his bed. There he remained all day, discussing in his mind the ways and means for executing a design that he had conceived.

"He didn't exactly say it would be a cheerful one," he mused. "He said merely that it wouldn't die. But it does worse than that. The gladiator wasn't haunted. It was simply dying – dying all the time. Well, I put it out of its misery. I'll have to do another thing like that. I'm going to kill that haunted automaton if I die in the attempt."

Such was his design. But he was not yet able to put it into execution. He tried his strength; he could hardly stand. The day wore away, and still he was too weak. He drank more brandy. Night finally came, and then he dreaded the undertaking in the dark.

Finally twelve o'clock struck; then one o'clock. The frightful visitors had quit creeping about the halls, and all had congregated in his room. He drank more. He became stronger, and there came to him a boldness born of desperation. Not another minute would he delay the annihilation of the haunted automaton. He got out of bed and lighted a candle. He knew where to find the hatchet with which he had put a stop to the sufferings of the dying gladiator, and he desired to use that particular hatchet in the deadly work that lay before him. It was in the rear part of the house. He found it. He went cautiously upstairs and approached the room of the haunted automaton. As he drew near to it he became more and more violently agitated – so much so, in fact, that when he pushed the door to enter the room the candle fell from his trembling hand and was instantly extinguished. He nerved himself with all his might, for he was determined to accomplish the work.

As he approached stealthily, step by step, he imagined he felt that maddening wink, and momentarily he expected to hear that unearthly voice declare, "I'm haunted." So, he decided to strike from the rear. He crept around and got behind the chair. He took one step forward, and that brought him just close enough. He raised the heavy hatchet in both hands, and with all the strength of a madman brought down its keen edge upon the head of his unconscious victim.

The automaton must have turned to air, for the blow fell upon empty space; and the strength that he had thrown into it precipitated him headlong into the automatons chair. But the haunted automaton was gone!

The old man, mad with terror and raving in delirium tremens, ran from the room, shrieking for help. He burst into Sarah's room. She was gone. He tore into Alice's room. She too was gone.

Yelling, screaming, raving, pursued by a thousand demons, desperately mad, he flew out of the house and down the street, shrieking "I'm haunted! I'm haunted! Help! Help!"

A policeman caught him and took him to prison. On Wednesday he was calm and rational, though somewhat ill and weak. A lawyer visited him at the hospital, whither he had been taken from jail, and handed him the following note, which the old man read several times before he could fully grasp its meaning:

My Dear Sir: I told you a few weeks ago that I should be married today, Wednesday, the 24th December. I have kept my word, as I was married an hour ago. If you want an automaton you may have that dummy that you saw in the back room of my workshop; for in reality that was the one you bought, and it has never left my shop. The money you paid me on account was just what I wanted to marry on. It is a little singular that when I told you I should marry today I had not even asked the girl! She never dreamed that such was my intention until last Saturday night, when I presented myself to her old servant, whose scream when she discovered me I greatly feared would betray my presence to a certain person who did not want me there. But the girl I wanted was sensible, and we made all necessary preparations and left the house Sunday. I feared that a certain person would hear our footfalls, though we went on tiptoes and as softly as possible.

That certain person was the girl's uncle. He had done me a bad turn, and I am now even with him; for not only did I frighten him out of his wits but I stole his niece from under his very nose and made him pay all the expenses of the wedding.

She is an excellent girl and is rich besides. By the way, her name is Alice and she is your niece; and as I am now her legal guardian, I desire that you should make to Mr. —— , the bearer of this, my attorney, a full accounting of all her property.

And by the way, further, we are to have a little dinner at our hotel this evening, at which our friends are expected. Can't you come? Do so, and let's be friends; for Christmas is a time when we should all make up. Hope you are better.

Howard Rankin, alias The Haunted Automaton.

The old man thought it all over – and went; and I am happy to add that he never drank another drop.

The Gloomy Shadow

My father enjoyed, among his other scientific attainments, a large family and an intimate acquaintance with the mysteries of phrenology. He was likewise an extremely methodical man, which is tantamount to saying that he was a conscientious man. There can be no conception of duty without a matured and coherent plan for its performance.

My father's principal idea of duty to his children found expression in the choice of proper vocations for them, and he based this choice upon careful phrenological analysis of their several heads. It is no small trick to be a good phrenologist. It involves intimate knowledge of cranial anatomy coupled with vast experience and intelligent observation. My father took his children in hand when they were yet of a very tender age and from a survey of their brain conformations he plotted their lives. Thus, to my eldest sister (next to whom I came in the order of introduction to life), he allotted the life pastime of teacher. For the brother who came next to me, both in sex and succession, he chose the distinction of the whistle and billy. To the next, a sister, he assigned the disagreeable task of a dutiful wife, and so on down to the very last chapter of this long reiteration of his personal heredity, with one exception, and that was I.

He had never diagnosticated my particular brain disease.

Why was it? I had asked myself that question a million times. I had asked my mother also, but she was a timid woman and contented herself with putting her arms around me and kissing me, and telling me that my father knew best, that I, being his first male offspring, probably was reserved for some very high walk in life. These puttings-off only half reassured me, for I knew that my father was a hard, though righteous, master in his own house, and that not a member of the family, from my mother down to the little two-year-old, whom my father already had set apart to disgrace the family as a politician, dared question his motives or suggest his policy.

Time passed, and yet my career had not been chosen. Of all the children I was the only one who had not been made up into a fire-cracker to explode at the proper time. I was becoming a big boy, with a violent tendency to legs. A white down was beginning to form upon my upper lip, and by this and other indications I knew that soon I should be a Man.

Why had my father neglected me? The more I thought about it the more mysterious his neglect became. I had arrived at an age when the human mind begins to operate of its own volition; when fancy runs riot and imagination is opening its eyes; when collar and cravat are ceasing to be nuisances, and the ripe sunset falls upon the willing eye; when the plaint of the whippoorwill in the twilight sets the soul a-dreaming, and the twinkling firefly kindles a spark of unrest; when Nature, after yawns interminable, rouses at last into wakefulness and folds us lovingly and caressingly in her warm embrace.

With adolescence comes, in a boy, strength; in a girl, tender-ness. I feared my father, but I loved him. Did he despise me? I knew an old lighting-blasted tree that always reminded me of my father. Tall and gaunt and thin it stood, and one gnarled branch remained; and if I looked at it from a certain point of view it seemed to be my father standing there in awful solitude, and with uplifted hand calling down the curse of heaven upon me; but if I got on the other side the expres-sion changed entirely, and the tree looked like my father invoking heaven's blessing upon me. Which point of view was it that marked my destiny? With boyish adolescence comes strength, and with strength independence. Why should I fear my father? He was a man – was not I also nearly a man? He had been kind to me all my life. He had laid violent hands upon me only once, and that was a long time ago, when he caught me trying to brain one of the little slaves with a heavy piece of iron; and then he whipped me till I was ill, and my mother cried a whole day because I was delirious and with a fever from the punishment. But I was a small boy then – what had I to fear now? I would go to my father and ask him to do for me what he had done for his other children.

Yet I hesitated. In the sharpened condition of my mental faculties I reflected upon some strange things I had seen and not understood. I had often detected my father watching me closely and with what I believed was a troubled look. When he would find that I had discovered him he would appear ashamed and more troubled yet. What did it mean? Had the gaunt old tree in the meadow cast its shadow upon me? Was it curses, or was it blessings? There must be light in order that shadows may exist. The gnarled branch pointed to heaven, whence light comes – and also curses.

Thus was I torn and racked. Discontent took up its habitation with me. Could not my father see that the flower was fading and the seed-pod ripening? He had dug the ground for the sowing, or would the seed be scattered among brambles and briars and strangled in the germination? I blamed my father – blamed him aloud to my mother; and I wish now that my tongue had been cut out for doing it.

There came the time when I could wait no longer. I went to my father and demanded, firmly but respectfully, as a duty from a father to a son, that he apply science to the laying out of a plan for my future conduct.

I shall never forget the profound astonishment, pain, anxiety and embarrassment that my father manifested when I made my demand. At first he showed anger, impatience and contempt, but these were succeeded by a pity that transfixed me, and then by a horror that drove me mad, my brain awhirl and ugly itching and turmoil rattling through my nerves. Quick and intelligent, he saw my rebellion, my exasperation, my wounded self-esteem, my turbulent blood surging, my jerking biceps, my grinding teeth, my rambling, unconscious and predatory finger-grasp, and then he was frightened and pale. I saw it plainly. Try as much as he would to conceal it, I saw it, I saw it! My father afraid of me! My father cowering before me, white and trembling! My father, a great, strong man, standing aghast before his puny son! My father, who had faced death with Scott in Mexico and who had fought like a tiger by Stonewall Jackson's side – this old soldier of a hundred battles, with a saber cut across his cheek, a man who could face the leveled pistol of an opposing duelist without the tremor of a nerve – this strong man, towering in manly strength and dignity and pride, stood a-bashed and fear-stricken before a miserable boy, his own son, whom a word or a blow would have sent cowering and howling away like a whipped dog!

What did it mean?

"Father," I demanded, "tell me what you mean.

"My son," said he, weakly and tremulously, "listen to your father. You are my eldest son. The honor of my name will rest upon your shoulders. Be content. Be manly. Respect your mother. Take life as you find it, and do the best you can for yourself and your mother and me. Be just to all. And mark you, my son: If ever temptation should assail you; if ever reason should feel inclined to succumb to passion; if ever the chains of wholesome restraint should be tugged at by the rash hand of Desire, then remember your mother –a good and gentle mother, who prays for you oftener than you dream of, who watches over you and loves you and imbues your circumstances with the tender essence of her sweet presence. Be her stay and comfort in her declining years. Let your arm gather the strength of trusty manhood, to be expended in shielding her from rough buffetings; and do not thus early in life permit Discontent to whisper in your ear vague longings that, being resonant, are empty, hollow and delusive. Go, my son."

It was the strangest speech I had heard in all my life. I left him, chilled to the marrow, sick at heart, touched by his appeal, but bewildered by the occasion of its delivery, numb of intellect, sore with puzzlings, and above all aching with a terror that, refusing to take shape and be torn out like an affronting eye, worked gnawingly at my vitals and stabbed me with invisible daggers.

What should I do? My mother was left to me – always a good mother, patient, kind and attentive. Did my father regard me as a monster? If so, did my mother also? She had given no sign of it – she had always been the same mother to me. Had she ever stood at the edge of the meadow and seen the riven tree calling down curses upon me, or had she ever gone to the other side where stood the giant old oak with the muscadine vine climbing to its summit and trying to strangle the very angel that bore it heavenward and seen the other and gender aspect?

I sought my mother without delay. Why did I? What was there in common between her sweet gentleness and my tumultuous unrest? Who can measure the strength of that mysterious and invisible cord which binds mother and son, though different as heaven and hell – this attenuated link, invisible as truth, impalpable as purity, inconceivable as right, impotent as strength, unimaginable as eternity? Can you weigh the odor of a rose? Would you measure off into rods, perches or poles the efficacy of a sigh, the aching of unsatisfied desire, the hope that feeds upon faith, the fondness that abides with possession, the longing of love, the grasping of affection, the tenderness born of fear, and, greater and grander than all, the community of hereditary instincts?

Where was my mother? I had lost no lime in seeking her. But where was she? She was not where I expected to find her – where I had been sure of finding her. She ought to have been sitting in her low wicker chair in the bay window of the family room, sewing, and now and then looking up at the clock to see if it was lime to order dinner. The little table, with innumerable and not understandable compartments, and mysterious nooks and corners, ought to have been just at her right elbow. Her embroidered footstool should have been in front of her chair, and her daintily slippered feet should have been resting upon it. The old Maltese cat, gray, wise and wicked, should have been curled up on the rug that the ottoman rested upon, utterly unconcerned over the ferocious aspect of the tiger's head on that end of the rug which was nearest the grate.

When I burst into the room my mother was not there!

What is superstition? What mean those whispered and unconscious deductions from the unusual? Snap a single cog in the machinery of life, and there ensue a bursting and a rattling and a banging that wake us up to the realization of living! Enjoyment is disturbance. There is life only in turmoil, in derangement of ordered things, in perversions of law. Hunt no further for the secret of the anarchist's existence, the scrambling of the politician, the source of ambition's whispering and sighing and wrangling down all the life-lighted avenues of human existence.

Where would be the pleasure of living were it not for the novelty of expected death?

She was not there. Then where was she? The old cat, warped with sin, obsequious as a Pharisee, patient as time, blinked at me – and kept a wary eye on my uncertain boot. The tiger's head yawned sleepily and impudently. The clock lacked thirty seconds of the time for ordering dinner.

My mother suddenly emerged from the parlor, the tall form of my father following. I saw the gaunt tree in the meadow calling down curses upon me. My mother was very pale. Her eyes wandered and her lips were white. She walked as in a dream – as in a nightmare, wherein skeletons and bloody flesh were busy disemboweling the repose of wistful sleep. She saw me. Had I gone to her and struck her in the face (God forgive the thought!) or stabbed her to the heart with a knife (Heaven blast me for the sacrilegious imagining!) she could not have been more sorely stricken than she was at beholding me. She looked at me in horror. Her eyes stared wildly.

Her lips, becoming purple, parted in desperate agony and fear; and, with upthrown hands and a cry that rang all the way down from destiny to death, she fell senseless to the floor.

She was my mother, and I loved her; but that unconscious glance of horror, that look of repulsion – blacker than night and deeper than hell – whence came it? The shadow of the tree had fallen upon her.

In what was I horrible? Was all repulsion centered in me, and did it blaze from my eyes, dribble from my finger-tips and exude from the pores of my skin? The tree came from the meadow into the room. With outstretched arm it pointed to the door and said:

"You have frightened your mother; go!"

The cat leered at me as I slunk away, and the tiger's head yawned with ineffable relief.

This mystery, this awful shadow, this impenetrable darkness, this enshrouding mist that enveloped me – whence came it? Whither would it lead me? Into what devious paths should I wander in its enfolding obscurity?

Science remained. Through the mist it beckoned dimly, beyond the darkness it faintly shone, above the shadow it loomed grim and immovable. Faith is the perverted longing for knowledge.

Learning is the cradle of despair. I would be rocked to sleep.

I knew a phrenologist who, like my father, was an able man. He did not know me – so much the better. I sought that man. It is a strange tale, my friends.

He was a professional phrenologist, and kept a shop where he examined heads for a moderate charge. He glanced at me only casually when I entered the room, because I was only a boy. (I have since learned that his principal business was the determination of occupations for those who already had chosen the course of their lives.) He was quite indifferent to me, but I am certain he was polite when he asked me to be seated.

I told him what I wanted. He laid his hands carelessly upon my head, but he had hardly done more than that when he sprang back and his face was livid with terror.

Here we were – we two – I a youth, he a man. It was not a large room. I was a strong lad. I walked to the door, locked it and put the key into my pocket.

There were only two of us – he and I. The blinding mist had come with me into the room, the shadow also was there and the darkness. I believe that through it all I saw the tall, lightning-blasted tree in the meadow. Only two of us and a mystery between us, the truth in his consciousness. I had strong arms. My fingers had a firm grasp and, no doubt, they could span the neck of an ordinary man. In my time I had squeezed the juice out of grapes and from the juice I had made wine and upon drinking the wine I had seen marvelous and enchanting visions that were sweeter than my hope of heaven.

I was calm about it at first, but I was bound to know what he knew –determined he should tell me what horrible thing my cranium revealed. I once had strangled a vicious dog – choked him till his tongue hung out and his eyes were ready to burst from their sockets, and then threw his carcass aside. I repeat that I was calm at first; but when he flatly refused to tell me, there came a strange kind of creeping into my arms – an intense accumulation of nervous force that clamored for exercise.

"Tell me!" I demanded, softly it is true, but the tone made him cower.

"I cannot," he cried.

"Tell me!" That creeping feeling in my arms was getting beyond control.

"Impossible!" he implored.

"It is too horrible!"

"Tell me!"

My hands had a peculiar way of opening and closing, and they felt desperate, hungry, empty.

"What do you wish to know?" asked the man, trying to put me off.

"I wish to know," I answered, still calmly, "what vocation I am suited for."

The creeping feeling in my arms was steadily assuming the more decided form of outreaching, and my fingers itched amazingly. He saw it.

"There is only one thing in life that you are fitted to be," he finally said, "and it pains me infinitely to add that it is the only thing which Nature in her inscrutable wisdom has decided that you cannot avoid being."

"And what is that?"

"A murderer!"

◆ ◆ ◆ ◆ ◆

My friends, what is destiny? For one, honor; for another, a rope. I do not complain. I love and respect Nature too much to whimper at her decrees. A gaunt lightning-stripped tree in a meadow, the plaint of a whippoorwill in the twilight, a Maltese cat sodden with crime, a sweet face blanched with horror – these are the microscopes with which gentle Nature provides us. (My dear sir, you are pulling that strap too hard – it hurts.) I am not talking for mercy or pity. Behold in me the infinite faith of one who loves Nature and bows to her law. (Keep the cap a moment longer, and then you may put it on me.) She marked out my life; I followed her inclination.

Farewell; may you all be happy as I am now in having fulfilled the destiny under which I was born! (Will that knot slip easily? There – but don't draw it too tight; my head won't slip through!)

The Haunted Burglar

Anthony Ross doubtless had the oddest and most complex temperament that ever assured the success of burglary as a business. This fact is mentioned in order that those who choose may employ it as an explanation of the extraordinary ideas that entered his head and gave a strangely tragic character to his career.

Though ignorant, the man had an uncommonly fine mind in certain aspect. Thus it happened that, while lacking moral perception, he cherished an artistic pride in the smooth, elegant, and finished conduct of his work. Hence a blunder on his part invariably filled him with grief and humiliation; and it was the steadily increasing recurrence of these errors that finally impelled him to make a deliberate analysis of his case.

Among the stupid acts with which he charged himself was the murder of the banker Uriah Mattson, a feeble old man whom a simple choking or a sufficient tap on the skull would have rendered helpless. Instead of that, he had choked his victim to death in the most brutal and unnecessary manner, and in doing so had used the fingers of his left hand in a singularly sprawled and awkward fashion. The whole act was utterly unlike him; it appalled and horrified him, – not for the sin of taking human life, but because it was unnecessary, dangerous, subversive of the principles of skilled burglary, and monstrously inartistic.

A similar mishap had occurred in the case of Miss Jellison, a wealthy spinster, merely because she was in the act of waking, which meant an ensuing scream. In this case, as in the other, he was unspeakably shocked to discover that the fatal choking had been done by the left hand, with sprawled and awkward fingers, and with a savage ferocity entirely uncalled for by his peril.

In setting himself to analyze these incongruous and revolting things he dragged forth from his memory numerous other acts, unlike those two in detail, but similar to them in spirit. Thus, in a fit of passionate anger at the whimpering of an infant, he had flung it brutally against the wall.

Another time he was nearly discovered through the needless torturing of a cat, whose cries set pursuers at his heels. These and other insane, inartistic, and ferocious acts he arrayed for serious analysis.

Finally the realization burst upon him that all his aberrations of conduct had proceeded from his left hand and arm. Search his recollection ever so diligently, he could not recall a single instance wherein his right hand had failed to proceed on perfectly fine, sure, and artistic lines.

When he made this discovery he realized that he had brought himself face to face with a terrifying mystery; and its horrors were increased when he reflected that while his left hand had committed acts of stupid atrocity in the pursuit of his burglarious enterprises, on many occasions when he was not so engaged it had acted with a less harmful but none the less coarse, irrational, and inartistic purpose.

It was not difficult for such a man to arrive at strange conclusions. The explanation that promptly suggested itself, and that his coolest and shrewdest wisdom could not shake, was that his left arm was under the dominion of a perverse and malicious spirit, that it was an entity apart from his own spirit, and that it had fastened itself upon that part of his body to produce his ruin.

It were useless, however inviting, to speculate upon the order of mind capable of arriving at such a conclusion; it is more to the point to narrate the terrible happenings to which it gave rise.

About a month after the burglar's mental struggle a strange-looking man applied for a situation at a saw-mill a hundred miles away. His appearance was exceedingly distressing. Either a grievous bodily illness or fearful mental anguish had made his face wan and haggard and filled his eyes with the light of a hard desperation that gave promise of dire results. There were no marks of a vagabond on his clothing or in his manner. He did not seem to be suffering for physical necessities. He held his head aloft and walked like a man, and an understanding glance would have seen that his look of determination meant something profounder and more far-reaching than the ordinary business concerns of life.

He gave the name of Hope. His manner was so engaging, yet withal so firm and abstracted, that he secured a position without difficulty; and so faithfully did he work, and so quick was his intelligence, that in good time his request to be given the management of a saw was granted. It might have been noticed that his face thereupon wore a deeper and more haggard look, but that its rigors were softened by a light of happy expectancy. As he cultivated no friendships among the men, he had no confidants; he went his dark way alone to the end.

He seemed to take more than the pleasure of an efficient workman in observing the products of his skill. He would stealthily hug the big brown logs as they approached the saw, and his eyes would blaze when the great tool went singing and roaring at its work. The foreman, mistaking this eagerness for carelessness, quietly cautioned him to beware; but when the next log was mounted for the saw the stranger appeared to slip and fall. He clasped the moving log in his arms, and the next moment the insatiable teeth had severed his left arm near the shoulder, and the stranger sank with a groan into the soft sawdust that filled the pit.

There was the usual commotion attending such accidents, for the faces of the workmen turn white when they see one of their number thus maimed for life. But Hope received good surgical care, and in due time was able to be abroad. Then the men observed that a remarkable change had come over him. His moroseness had disappeared, and in its stead was a hearty cheer of manner that amazed them. Was the losing of a precious arm a thing to make a wretched man happy? Hope was given light work in the office, and might have remained to the end of his days a competent and prosperous man; but one day he left, and was never seen thereabout again.

Then Anthony Ross, the burglar, reappeared upon the scenes of his former exploits. The police were dismayed to note the arrival of a man whom all their skill had been unable to convict of terrible crimes which they were certain he had committed, and they questioned him about the loss of his arm; but he laughed them away with the fine old sangfroid with which they were familiar, and soon his handiwork appeared in reports of daring burglaries.

A watch of extraordinary care and minuteness was set upon him, but that availed nothing until a singular thing occurred to baffle the officers beyond measure: Ross had suddenly become wildly reckless and walked red-handed into the mouth of the law. By evidence that seemed indisputable a burglary and atrocious murder were traced to him. Stranger than all else, he made no effort to escape, though leaving a hanging trail behind him. When the officers overhauled him, they found him in a state of utter dejection, wholly different from the lighthearted bearing that had characterized him ever since he had returned without his left arm. Neither admitting nor denying his guilt, he bore himself with the hopelessness of a man already condemned to the gallows.

Even when he was brought before a jury and placed on trial, he made no fight for his life.

Although possessed of abundant means, he refused to employ an attorney, and treated with scant courtesy the one assigned him by the judge. He betrayed irritation at the slow dragging of the case as the prosecution piled up its evidence against him. His whole manner indicated that he wished the trial to end as soon as possible and hoped for a verdict of guilty.

This incomprehensible behavior placed the voting and ambitious attorney on his mettle. He realized that some inexplicable mystery lay behind the matter, and this sharpened his zeal to find it. He plied his client with all manner of questions, and tried in all way to secure his confidence:

Ross remained sullen, morose, and wholly given over to despairing resignation. The young lawyer had made a wonderful discovery, which he at first felt confident would clear the prisoner, but any mention of it to Ross would only throw him into a violent passion and cause him to tremble as with a palsy. His conduct on such occasions was terrible beyond measure. He seemed utterly beside himself, and thus his attorney had become convinced of the man's insanity. The trouble in proving it was that he dared not mention his discovery to others, and that Ross exhibited no signs of mania unless that one subject was broached.

The prosecution made out a case that looked impregnable, and this fact seemed to fill the prisoner with peace. The young lawyer for the defense had summoned a number of witnesses, but in the end he used only one. His opening statement to the jury was merely that it was a physical impossibility for the prisoner to have committed the murder, – which was done by choking. Ross made a frantic attempt to stop him from putting forth that defense, and from the dock wildly denounced it as a lie.

The young lawyer nevertheless proceeded with what he deemed his duty to his unwilling client. He called a photographer and had him produce a large picture of the murdered man's face and neck. He proved that the portrait was that of the person whom Ross was charged with having killed. As he approached the climax of the scene, Ross became entirety ungovernable in his frantic efforts to stop the introduction of the evidence, and so it became necessary to bind and gag him and strap him to the chair.

When quiet was restored, the lawyer handed the photograph to the jury and quietly remarked:

"You may see for yourselves that the choking was done with the left hand, and you have observed that my client has no such member."

He was unmistakably right. The imprint of the thumb and fingers, forced into the flesh in a singularly ferocious, sprawling, and awkward manner, was shown in the photograph with absolute clearness. The prosecution, taken wholly by surprise, blustered and made attempts to assail the evidence, but without success. The jury returned a verdict of not guilty.

Meanwhile the prisoner had fainted, and his gag and bonds had been removed; but he recovered at the moment when the verdict was announced. He staggered to his feet, and his eyes rolled; then with a thick tongue he exclaimed:

"It was the left arm that did it! This one" – holding his right arm as high as he could reach –"never made a mistake. It was always the left one. A spirit of mischief and murder was in it. I cut it off in a saw-mill, but the spirit stayed where the arm used to be, and it choked this man to death. I didn't want you to acquit me. I wanted you to hang me. I can't go through life having this thing haunting me and spoiling my business and making a murderer of me. It tries to choke me while I sleep. There it is! Can't you see it?" And he looked with wide-staring eves at his left side.

"Mr. Sheriff," gravely said the judge, "take this man before the Commissioners of Lunacy tomorrow."

The Faithful Amulet

A quaint old rogue, who called himself Rabaya, the Mystic, was one of the many extraordinary characters of that odd corner of San Francisco known as the Latin Quarter. His business was the selling of charms and amulets, and his generally harmless practices received an impressive aspect from his Hindu parentage, his great age, his small, wizened frame, his deeply wrinkled face, his outlandish dress, and the barbaric fitting of his den.

One of his most constant customers was James Freeman, the half-piratical owner and skipper of the "Blue Crane." This queer little barkentine, of light tonnage but wonderful sailing qualities, is remembered in every port between Sitka and Callao. All sorts of strange stories are told of her exploits, but these mostly were manufactured by superstitious and highly imaginative sailors, who commonly demonstrate the natural affinity existing between idleness and lying. It has been said not only that she engaged in smuggling, piracy, and "blackbirding" (which is kidnapping Gilbert Islanders and selling them to the coffee-planters of Central America), but that she maintained special relations with Satan, founded on the power of mysterious charms which her skipper was supposed to have procured from some mysterious source and was known to employ on occasion. Beyond the information which his manifests and clearance papers divulged, nothing of his supposed shady operations could be learned either from him or his crew; for his sailors, like him, were a strangely silent lot – all sharp, keen-eyed young fellows who never drank and who kept to themselves when in port. An uncommon circumstance was that there were never any vacancies in the crew, except one that happened as the result of Freeman's last visit to Rabaya, and it came about in the following remarkable manner:

Freeman, like most other men who follow the sea, was superstitious, and he ascribed his fair luck to the charms which he secretly procured from Rabaya. It is now known that he visited the mystic whenever he came to the port of San Francisco, and there are some today who believe that Rabaya had an interest in the supposed buccaneering enterprises of the "Blue Crane."

Among the most intelligent and active of the "Blue Crane's" crew was a Malay known to his mates as the Flying Devil. This had come to him by reason of his extraordinary agility. No monkey could have been more active than he in the rigging; he could make flying leaps with astonishing ease. He could not have been more than twenty-five years old, but he had the shriveled appearance of an old man, and was small and lean. His face was smooth-shaved and wrinkled, his eyes deep set and intensely black and brilliant. His mouth was his most forbidding feature. It was large, and the thin lips were drawn tightly over large and protruding teeth, its aspect being prognathous and menacing. Although quiet and not given to laughter, at times he would smile, and then the expression of his face was such as to give even Freeman a sensation of impending danger.

It was never clearly known what was the real mission of the "Blue Crane" when she sailed the last time from San Francisco. Some supposed that she intended to loot a sunken vessel of her treasure; others that the enterprise was one of simple piracy, involving the killing of the crew and the scuttling of the ship in mid-ocean; others that a certain large consignment of opium, for which the customs authorities were on the lookout, was likely to be smuggled into some port of Puget Sound. In any event, the business ahead must have been important, for it is now known that in order to ensure its success Freeman bought an uncommonly expensive and potent charm from Rabaya.

When Freeman went to buy this charm he failed to notice that the Flying Devil was slyly following him; neither he nor the half-blind charm-seller observed the Malay slip into Rabaya's den and witness the matter that there went forward. The intruder must have heard something that stirred every evil instinct in him. Rabaya (whom I could hardly be persuaded to believe under oath) years afterward told me that the charm which he sold to Freeman was one of extraordinary virtue. For many generations it had been in the family of one of India's proudest rajahs, and until it was stolen the arms of England could not prevail over that part of the far East. If borne by a person of lofty character (as he solemnly informed me he believed Freeman to be) it would never fail to bring the highest good fortune; for, although the amulet was laden with evil powers as well as good, a worthy person could resist the evil and employ only the good. Contrariwise, the amulet in the hands of an evil person would be a most potent and dangerous engine of harm.

It was a small and very old trinket, made of copper and representing a serpent twined grotesquely about a human heart; through the heart a dagger was thrust, and the loop for holding the suspending string was formed by one of the coils of the snake. The charm had a wonderful history, which must be reserved for a future story; the sum of it being that as it had been as often in the hands of bad men as of good, it had wrought as many calamities as blessings. It was perfectly safe and useful – so Rabaya soberly told me – in the hands of such a man as Freeman.

Now, as no one knows the soundings and breadth of his own wickedness, the Flying Devil (who, Rabaya, explained, must have overheard the conversation attending its transference to Freeman) reflected only that if he could secure possession of the charm his fortune would be made; as he could not procure it by other means, he must steal it. Moreover, he must have seen the price – five thousand dollars in gold – which Freeman paid for the trinket; and that alone was sufficient to move the Malay's cupidity. At all events, it is known that he set himself to steal the charm and desert from the barkentine.

From this point on to the catastrophe my information is somewhat hazy. I cannot say, for instance, just how the theft was committed, but it is certain that Freeman was not aware of it until a considerable time had passed. What did concern him particularly was the absence of the Malay when the barkentine was weighing anchor and giving line for a tow out to sea. The Malay was a valuable sailor; to replace him adequately was clearly so impossible a task that Freeman decided, after a profitless and delaying search of hours, to leave port without him or another in his place.

It was with a heavy heart, somewhat lightened by a confident assumption that the amulet was safe in his possession, that Freeman headed down the channel for the Golden Gate.

Meanwhile, the Flying Devil was having strange adventures. In a hastily arranged disguise, the principal feature of which was a gentleman's street dress, in which he might pass careless scrutiny as a thrifty Japanese awkwardly trying to adapt himself to the customs of his environment, he emerged from a water-front lodging-house of the poorer sort, and ascended leisurely to the summit of Telegraph Hill, in order to make a careful survey of the city from that prominent height; for it was needful that he know how best to escape. From that alluring eminence he saw not only a great part of the city, but also nearly the whole of the bay of San Francisco and the shores, town, and mountains lying beyond. His first particular attention was given to the "Blue Crane," upon which he looked nearly straight down as she rolled gently at her moorings at the foot of Lombard Street. Two miles to the west he saw the trees which conceal the soldier's barracks, and the commanding general's residence on the high promontory known as Black Point, and these invited him to seek concealment in their shadows until the advent of night would enable him to work his way down the peninsula of San Francisco to the distant blue mountains of San Mateo. Surmising that Freeman would make a search for him, and that it would be confined to the docks and their near vicinity, he imagined that it would not be a difficult matter to escape.

After getting his bearings the Malay was in the act of descending the hill by its northern flank, when he observed a stranger leaning against the parapet crowning the hill. The man seemed to be watching him. Not reflecting that his somewhat singular appearance might have accounted for the scrutiny, his suspicions were roused; he feared, albeit wrongly, that he was followed, for the stranger had come up soon after him. Assuming an air of indifference, he strolled about until he was very near the stranger, and then with the swiftness and ferocity of a tiger he sprang and slipped a knife-blade between the man's ribs. The stranger sank with a groan, and the Malay fled down the hill.

It was a curious circumstance that the man fell in front of one of the openings which neglect had permitted the rains to wash underneath the parapet. He floundered as some dying men will, and these movements caused him to work his body through the opening. That done, he started rolling down the steep eastern declivity, the speed of his flight increasing with every bound.

Many cottages are perched precariously on this precipitous slope. Mrs. Armour, a resident of one of them, was sitting in a rear room near the window, sewing, when she was amazed to see a man flying through the sash close beside her. He came with so great violence that he tore through a thin partition into an adjoining room and landed in a shapeless heap against the opposite wall.

Mrs. Armour screamed for help. A great commotion ensued, but it was some time before the flight of the body was connected with a murder on the parapet. Nevertheless, the police were active, and presently a dozen of them were upon the broad trail which the murderer had left in his flight down the hill.

In a short time the Malay found himself in the lumber-piles of the northern water-front.

Thence, after gathering himself together, he walked leisurely westward in the rear of the wire-works, and traversed a little sand-beach where mothers and nurses had children out for an airing.

The desperate spirit of perversity which possessed the man (and which Rabaya afterwards explained by the possession of the amulet), made reckless by a belief that the charm which he carried would preserve him from all menaces, led him to steal a small hand-satchel that lay on the beach near a well-dressed woman. He walked away with it, and then opened it and was rejoiced to find that it contained some money and fine jewelry. At this juncture one of the children, who had observed the Malay's theft, called the woman's attention to him. She started in pursuit, raising a loud outcry, which emptied the adjacent drinking-saloons of a pursuing crowd.

The Malay leaped forward with ample ability to outstrip all his pursuers, but just as he arrived in front of a large swimming establishment a bullet from a policeman's pistol brought him to his knees. The crowd quickly pressed around him. The criminal staggered to his feet, made a fierce dash at a man who stood in his way, and sank a good knife into his body. Then he bounded away, fled swiftly past a narrow beach where swimming clubs have their houses, and disappeared in the ruins of a large old building that lay at the foot of a sandy bluff on the water's edge. He was trailed a short distance within the ruins by a thin stream of blood which he left, and there he was lost. It was supposed that he had escaped to the old woolen-mill on Black Point As in all other cases where a mob pursues a fleeing criminal, the search was wild and disorderly, so that if the Malay had left any trail beyond the ruins it would have been obliterated by trampling feet. Only one policeman was in the crowd, but others, summoned by telephone, were rapidly approaching from all directions. Unintelligent and contradictory rumors bewildered the police for a time, but they formed a long picket line covering an arc which stretched from North Beach to the new gas-works far beyond Black Point.

It was about this time that Captain Freeman cast off and started out to sea.

The summit of Black Point is crowned with the tall eucalyptus trees which the Flying Devil had seen from Telegraph Hill. A high fence, which encloses the general's house, extends along the bluff of Black Point, near the edge. A sentry paced in front of the gate to the grounds, keeping out all who had not provided themselves with a pass. The sentry had seen the crowd gathering towards the east, and in the distance he noticed the brass buttons of the police glistening in the western sunlight. He wondered what could be afoot.

While he was thus engaged he observed a small, dark, wiry man emerging upon the bluff from the direction of the woolen-mill at its eastern base. The stranger made straight for the gate.

"You can't go in there," said the soldier, "unless you have a pass."

"Da w'at?" asked the stranger.

"A pass," repeated the sentry; and then, seeing that the man was a foreigner and imperfectly acquainted with English, he made signs to explain his remark, still carrying his bayonet-tipped rifle at shoulder-arms. The stranger, whose sharp gleam of eye gave the soldier an odd sensation, nodded and smiled.

"Oh!" said he; "I have."

He thrust his hand into his side-pocket, advancing meanwhile, and sending a swift glance about. In the next moment the soldier found himself sinking to the ground with an open jugular.

The Malay slipped within the grounds and disappeared in the shrubbery. It was nearly an hour afterwards that the soldier's body was discovered, and, the crowd of police and citizens arriving, it became known to the garrison that the desperate criminal was immediately at hand. The bugle sounded and the soldiers came tumbling out of barracks. Then began a search of every corner of the post.

It is likely that a feeling of relief came to many a stout heart when it was announced that the man had escaped by water, and was now being swiftly carried down the channel towards the Golden Gate by the ebb tide. He was clearly seen in a small boat, keeping such a course as was possible by means of a rude board in place of oars. His escape had occurred thus: Upon entering the grounds he ran along the eastern fence, behind the shrubbery, to a transverse fence separating the garden from the rear premises. He leaped the fence, and then found himself face to face with a large and formidable mastiff. He killed the brute in a strange and bold manner – by choking.

There was evidence of a long and fearful struggle between man and brute. The apparent reason for the man's failure to use the knife was the first necessity of choking the dog into silence and the subsequent need of employing both hands to maintain that advantage.

After disposing of the dog the Flying Devil, wounded though he was, performed a feat worthy of his sobriquet; he leaped the rear fence. At the foot of the bluff he found a boat chained to a post and sunk into the sand. There was no way to release the boat except by digging up the post.

This the Malay did with his hands for tools, and then threw the post into the boat, and pushed off with a board that he found on the beach. Then he swung out into the tide, and it was some minutes afterwards that he was discovered from the fort; and then he was so far away, and there was so much doubt of his identity, that the gunners hesitated for a time to fire upon him. Then two dramatic things occurred.

Meeting the drifting boat was a heavy bank of fog which was rolling through the Golden Gate.

The murderer was heading straight for it, paddling vigorously with the tide. If once the fog should enfold him he would be lost in the Pacific or killed on the rocks almost beyond a peradventure, and yet he was heading for such a fate with all the strength that he possessed. This was what first convinced his pursuers that he was the man whom they sought – none other would have pursued so desperate a course. At the same time a marine glass brought conviction, and the order was given to open fire.

A six-pound brass cannon roared, and splinters flew from the boat; but its occupant, with tantalizing bravado, rose and waved his hands defiantly. The six-pounder then sent out a percussion shell, and just as the frail boat was entering the fog it was blown into a thousand fragments. Some of the observers swore positively that they saw the Malay floundering in the water a moment after the boat was destroyed and before he was engulfed by the fog, but this was deemed incredible. In a short time the order of the post had been restored and the police had taken themselves away.

The other dramatic occurrence must remain largely a matter of surmise, but only because the evidence is so strange.

The great steel gun employed at the fort to announce the setting of the sun thrust its black muzzle into the fog. Had it been fired with shot or shell its missile would have struck the hills on the opposite side of the channel. But the gun was never so loaded; blank cartridges were sufficient for its function. The bore of the piece was of so generous a diameter that a child or small man might have crept into it had such a feat ever been thought of or dared.

There are three circumstances indicating that the fleeing man escaped alive from the wreck of his boat, and that he made a safe landing in the fog on the treacherous rocks at the foot of the bluff crowned by the guns. The first of these was suggested by the gunner who fired the piece that day, two or three hours after the destruction of the fleeing man's boat; and even that would have received no attention under ordinary circumstances, and, in fact, did receive none at all until long afterwards, when Rabaya reported that he had been visited by Freeman, who told him of the two other strange circumstances. The gunner related that when he fired the cannon that day he discovered that it recoiled in a most unaccountable manner, as though it had been loaded with something in addition to a blank cartridge. But he had loaded the gun himself, and was positive that he placed no shot in the barrel. At that time he was utterly unable to account for the recoil.

The second strange occurrence came to my knowledge through Rabaya. Freeman told him that as he was towing out to sea that afternoon he encountered a heavy fog immediately after turning from the bay into the channel. The tow-boat had to proceed very slowly. When his vessel had arrived at a point opposite Black Point he heard the sunset gun, and immediately afterwards strange particles began to fall upon the barkentine, which was exactly in the vertical plane of the gun's range. He had sailed many waters and had seen many kinds of showers, but this was different from all others. Fragments of a sticky substance fell all over the deck, and clung to the sails and spars where they touched them. They seemed to be finely shredded flesh, mixed with particles of shattered bone, with a strip of cloth here and there; and the particles that looked like flesh were of a blackish red and smelled of powder. The visitation gave the skipper and his crew a "creepy" sensation, and awed them somewhat – in short, they were depressed by the strange circumstance to such an extent that Captain Freeman had to employ stern measures to keep down a mutiny, so fearful were the men of going to sea under that terrible omen.

The third circumstance is equally singular. As Freeman was pacing the deck and talking reassuring to his crew his foot struck a small, grimy, metallic object lying on the deck. He picked it up and discovered that it, too, bore the odor of burned powder. When he had cleaned it he was amazed to discover that it was the amulet which he had bought that very day from Rabaya. He could not believe it was the same until he had made a search and found that it had been stolen from his pocket.

It needs only to be added that the Flying Devil was never seen afterwards.

The Woman of the Inner Room

Dr. Osborne, hastily summoned to the receiving hospital, found there a handsome, well-dressed young man with an ugly hole in his skull about an inch and a half above the left ear. The injured man evidently was not suffering, but the desperate nature of his hurt was seen in the deep pallor of his face. His expression was placid, unintelligent, and absolutely silly. Yet he was freely alive – his breathing was good, his heart observed its functions, his temperature was normal, and his skin was warm and moist. Dr. Osborne cleared the wound with a sponge.

"How was the lad hurt?" he asked of the officers who were standing about.

No one could tell. A few minutes ago some one had seen him staggering along the street, clinging to the house-walls to keep from falling, a thin stream of blood trickling down his face, and had pointed him out to a policeman.

Dr. Osborne looked closely at the wound. Then he tried to insert a finger in the opening, but failed. He looked around upon the men, and asked them to show him their hands.

"No," he said, after examining them; "your fingers are all too blunt Farley, go and call my daughter – she is sitting in my buggy at the door."

Before she came, Dr. Osborne asked:

"Do you know who he is?"

None could inform him. Not a scrap of paper by which he might be identified could be found upon him.

The surgeon's daughter entered. She was an attractive girl – rather tall and slight, had brown eyes and hair, and carried herself with a fine unconscious grace. She glanced at the man lying on the operating-table, suddenly checked her advance, and became pale. Her father, with a reassuring manner, took her by the arm, and led her forward.

"Don't be alarmed, Agnes," he said; "I have tested your nerve before, and have never seen it fail. Let me see your hand." He took it in his and examined it closely. "That is just what I need. "

he resumed; "long, slender fingers – you have a beautiful hand, Agnes."

This embarrassed her, but she became stronger.

"Now, my child, I must learn the nature of the wound in this young man's head. Come a little closer, my dear; he does not know what is going on. Have you ever seen him before?"

"No," she replied, approaching nearer and regarding his face steadily; "but he appears to be a man of means and refinement."

"Yes; that is clear. But come closer, Agnes. Why, you are all right! You see, it is a small hole, and that probably accounts for the fact that he is still alive; but it has penetrated the skull, and that makes the case a very serious one. It is necessary that I know what made the wound, in order to determine what to do; and the quickest way in the world is to let the wound tell its own story. My fingers are so thick that I can do nothing. Yours are exactly suited."

"My fingers? What do you want me to do, father?"

"I want you to insert a finger in the wound and tell me what you find, after a careful examination of the edges of the bone."

The girl hesitated. "But – why?" she asked.

"So that I may know what instrument was employed, if the hole is round and has rather clean edges, it was made by a bullet – in which event, there is no reasonable hope of recovery, If, however, it is three-cornered, or otherwise angular, or in any great degree ragged, then something else made it – a pick-axe or some other instrument; and in that case there is a bare chance of saving his life. Besides, the knowledge will be very useful to the officers in digging up what appears to be a mysterious crime. You can ascertain that, can't you?"

"I will try."

Under her father's direction, but in a gingerly manner, she stood behind the young man's head, her face close above his, and put the fine, long forefinger of her left hand into the wound. As she did so, her eyes met the empty stare of his. Very slowly and carefully, watching his face all the time, she felt the edges of the bone and then withdrew her finger.

"It is smooth and round," she said.

"Ah!" exclaimed her father; "then there is no hope, poor fellow! But let us try a little further Agnes, my dear, you did that bravely, as I knew you would: but now I want you to put your finger in again, and push it very slowly and carefully as far as you can. The bullet may not have gone far."

The girl, again looking down upon the calm, peaceful face, with its blank stare and senseless smile, explored the wound with her finger. Her touch was sure and gentle, but as her finger came in contact with the brain, and she felt its warmth and the regular and smooth pressure of the pulsations, her nerves went upon a strain. Still she looked down into the handsome young face, but she was growing pale. All of a sudden, for some wholly unaccountable reason, the young man's blank expression and silly smile passed away, and a certain intelligence sat upon his fare.

The surgeon saw this, and it appeared to him to be a matter of uncommon importance. At the same moment, a peculiar look came into his daughter's face. She had begun to relax in the course of fainting, but instantly she swung back upon a nervous balance which was so prominent as to suggest a strong stimulation. The young man looked up into her eyes with a vague interest; she looked down into his with fear and horror. Then she suddenly withdrew her finger and stepped back beyond the range of his vision. The look of vacuity again took a hold upon him.

The girl, without addressing any one particularly, said, nervously and hurriedly; "You had better send to the bank and tell his father."

"What bank?" asked her father, in surprise.

"The Citizens' Bank."

"Who is his father?"

"Mr. Blanchard, the president of the bank. This is his son, Charles."

Her father regarded her with amazement, but he refrained from asking her questions. He merely remarked; "But you said just now that you did not know him."

The girl looked confused and made no reply.

The surgeon sent an officer to the bank. His attention returned to the patient, and as his daughter had not made as thorough an examination as he desired, he asked her if she felt strong enough to make another attempt. She complied, but with much hesitation. Again did a sickness and weakness assail her as her finger slipped into the wound, and again did the young man's face brighten. He fixed his eyes on her face, seemingly in recognition, and in a thick, stammering voice, he said:

"Why, Agnes, is it you? So, you are the one – this is what jealousy has done. This is what I get for being his friend."

"Do you blame me, Charles?"

"Why should I? It is too late for that now."

"Does Frank know?"

"He does not; but she is madly in love with him."

"And she is a stranger to you?"

"Absolutely. I never saw her before. I believe he has her in hiding, and that he will shield her."

"But he is not a traitor."

"She may have some unaccountable hold upon him."

"He would not deceive me so."

"Who can tell?"

The excitement which had kept back the encroachment of weakness now failed of purpose.

The girl withdrew her finger, and the young man sank back into his former lethargic condition.

All color fled the girl's face; her eyes were fixed vacantly in a stare of horror.

"Agnes," said her father, approaching her hastily, "what is the matter? Are you faint?"

"I – I don't know, father." She trembled, as though with apoplexy.

"What is all this he has been telling you?" he asked.

She was too far gone to reply, but her father mistook her weakness for hesitation.

"Come into the open air, my child. This repulsive ordeal and the ravings of that delirious man have borne too heavily upon your nerves. Come, my daughter."

Those were his words, but a great dread had arisen within him. As soon as they had stepped without, he pressed the question upon her with a certain hardness which came from his anxiety:

"What does all this mean? What do you know about the shooting?"

Her voice was kept back by a gasp, and with a lurch she slipped from her father's grasp and went all disorganized down to the ground before he could save her. He picked her up, placed her in the buggy, and drove rapidly to his home. When she recovered she found her mother in anxious watch upon her, for her father had gone to see what could be done for the wounded man.

Mrs. Osborne had been informed by her husband of the singular occurrence at the receiving hospital, and the good woman was unhappy over it. But with her usual fair tact she asked no questions, believing that the close understanding between her and her daughter would bring forth an explanation in safe time. She was disappointed, therefore, when Agnes, upon coming into consciousness, spoke no word of the most important matter. More than that, she said she had a grievous headache and desired to be left alone, that she might sleep. Mrs. Osborne withdrew, and immediately the girl went about the task of slipping away from the house unseen. She did this with whole success. In a few minutes she was in the office of a young physician named Frank Armour.

There was nothing commonplace in this young man's appearance. He was tall, slender, and pale, and to the manifest effects of rigorous study were added evidences of some kind of trouble that was wearing him out. He occupied two rooms – a reception-room and, behind it, a consultation-room. She found him sitting in the front room; the door leading into the other was closed. His face brightened greatly when he saw her standing before him.

"Agnes'" he cried; "I am very glad to see you. All loads drop from my shoulders when your sweet face appears. You said the other day that you were not coming to the office any more, for fear people would talk about you – as though that should make any difference, seeing that we are soon to be married!"

His manner was so gentle, so full of evidences of genuine affection, that her suspicions concerning him were much weakened. But she had come to make sure of her position, and the mysteries of the wounded man's speech had to be cleared up.

"Frank," she asked, "have you seen your friend Charles Blanchard today?"

"No; I haven't seen him since last night. By the way, he scolded me again for not taking him around to your house and introducing him to you. Now, really, Agnes, I don't think you ought to keep putting me off about bringing him, as he is really a very delightful man, and I am sure you will like him."

"We will talk about that some other time, Frank. There is something else I want to ask you now. Do you really think you love me and me alone?"

"I am very certain of it, Agnes; but I don't see any reason for such a question."

"I know that you never go into society, and you have told me that you pay attentions to no one except me."

"That is the truth, Agnes; but to save my life I don't understand you. You are pale and ill. Something has happened to give you trouble and you have suddenly become suspicious of me."

Should she tell him of the fatal wounding of his best friend? Was it not possible first to extort from him some explanation of that friend's singular disclosures? The fact that she had received this knowledge from him – if, indeed, knowledge it was – troubled her greatly. The man had sown distrust in her mind, and it was like poison.

"Frank," she said, presently, unable to see him longer in ignorance of his friend's condition, "Charles Blanchard has been seriously hurt, and I came to tell you so."

"Seriously hurt?" asked Armour, in alarm; "when and how?"

"He was found less than two hours ago and taken to the receiving hospital, where my father is attending him now."

The young physician was now upon his feet, nervous and excited.

"How was he hurt, Agnes? Tell me all about it."

"Nothing is known except that he was found staggering along the street with a pistol wound in the head."

Armour's face was livid, and his trembling legs nearly failed to support his weight.

"He was not killed instantly?" he asked.

"No; but he is unconscious."

"Certainly."

"The bullet must have been a small one."

"No doubt, no doubt!" cried the unhappy man; "I must go to see him at once."

He picked up his hat and was starting away, expecting her to leave the room with him. But she sat still, remarking:

"I will wait until you return, if you promise to come back soon."

Armour's disappointment and annoyance were visibly manifest. He shot a quick glance toward the door of the adjoining room, and then walked over to it and cautiously tried the knob. The door was locked. He made a show of feeling in his pocket for the key, but his whole manner was so openly embarrassed that the sharp-sighted girl noticed it.

"Agnes," said he, turning upon her somewhat impatiently, "there is no doubt I shall be gone a long time, and it would be unreasonable for me to ask you to wait."

"Nevertheless," she said, in rather a hard tone, looking him steadily in the eyes, "I will stay here and wait for you. If you stay away long I will turn on the spring-latch and thus lock the door when I leave."

An evident fear seized upon the young physician. He was anxious to go to his suffering friend, and was unwilling to leave Agnes in his office. She saw all this very plainly.

"And, by the way, Frank," she resumed, "as I am very tired, I will go into the back room and rest on the lounge." She started toward the door, pretending not to have noticed that it was locked, and tried to open it.

"Why, it is locked!" she exclaimed.

Armour's uneasiness had increased to positive suffering.

"Yes" he stammered.

"Is any one in there?"

"Agnes – Well?"

"You are acting in a strange and unaccountable way today."

"I?" she asked, in great astonishment; "I don't understand you, Frank." Then she walked straight up to him, and, placing her hands on his shoulders, said, with dignity and tenderness: "I merely asked you if there was any one in the room, and you are offended. Let us be candid with each other, Frank. What does it mean?"

"I may have a patient in that room, and–". A low moaning in a woman's voice, indistinctly heard from the inner room, interrupted him, His faced turned scarlet and then pale, and all the time the steady gaze of the surgeon's daughter was upon him. She took her hands from his shoulders, looking much humiliated; and, with a painful sadness which he had never before seen in her conduct, she simply said:

"I don't think it is customary for physicians to lock their patients up; but if I have been rude I beg you to forgive me. I will not annoy you by staying. Good-bye, Frank."

She extended her hand, which he seized eagerly; but she quickly withdrew it and left the room.

He followed her into the passage-way.

"Agnes," he said "you surely don't suspect that" – but she was fleeing down the stairs so rapidly that he could not finish the foolish sentence.

The girl went so quickly along the crowded street that people turned in wonder to look at her.

Her eyes were filled with tears, her face was very pale, and her lips were tightly caught between her teeth. "I never would have dreamed it," she said to herself, over and over; "never, never, never! Oh, it will kill me, it will kill me!" She reentered her home as secretly as she had left it, flung herself wearily upon her bed, and cried as though her heart was broken.

The police had gone intelligently to work upon the mystery of the shooting. Mr. Blanchard, the father of the wounded man, had arrived, overcome with grief and horror. Dr. Armour, he said, was the only intimate friend his son had. He was entirely unable to suggest any cause for the shooting, which undoubtedly had not been done with a suicidal hand. The police repeated to him all that they could remember of the disjointed and unintelligible conversation between his son and Agnes Osborne, and this account puzzled him sorely. What mysterious blind was there between his son and this young woman? She had denied all knowledge of him, and yet she gave the information of his identity. When and how had he been her friend, not knowing her? Why had she discovered an anxiety that he should not blame her for the deed that would cost him his life? Why was she desirous of learning from him whether Frank Armour knew anything about the tragedy? Who was this that was madly in love with Armour, and what possible connection could there be between this fact and that of the shooting? Who was the woman referred to in their conversation, and why should Armour keep her in hiding? How could her jealousy of young Blanchard be the moving cause of the desperate assault?

Mr. Blanchard was not the only one who tried to bring some light out of the darkness of all this singular and deplorable transaction. A broken-hearted girl, tossing and weeping on her bed, asked herself these questions, or some of them, many times, and the police were weighing them with all the care and precision of trained hunters of crime, With Dr. Osborne the matter was far more serious than with the police. Lacking his knowledge that the young man's temporary restoration to a state of consciousness was not explainable on ordinary grounds, they did not see the true value of the fact Dr. Osborne reasoned that a wound of that character must necessarily produce a disorganization of the mental functions and present a condition of unconsciousness This had been the case until his daughter had inserted her finger far into the wound, when at once the sufferer's face brightened and a condition resembling consciousness ensued. Dr. Osborne was too wise to assume that young Blanchard's ability to speak and apparently carry forward a conversation was positive evidence of consciousness, for he knew that the vagaries of a disorganized mind are of unimaginable variety. But this case was unique – nothing in the books or his experience had a suggestion of its form or color. The whole case was this: His daughter had betrayed fright upon seeing the wounded man at the station, but had recovered from that; and, indeed, her condition might have been construed as one of natural repugnance, overcome by an intelligent direction of the will. It was clear enough so far. When she placed her finger in the edge of the wound there was sign neither of recognition on her part nor consciousness on his; it was only when she had pushed her finger into the brain that those two facts came into existence.

This appeared to the surgeon to be a very strange coincidence. Not only was the young man apparently restored to consciousness, but the two, supposed to have been strangers, recognized each other, and, worse than all else, betrayed a certain ill-defined common knowledge of the crime. All these things threw Dr. Osborne into the most conflicting surmises and brought him into a condition of positive unhappiness. The extraordinary scientific features of the case were overshadowed by his anxieties, His daughter had engaged herself, with his assent, to marry Dr.

Armour, and yet this young physician had been placed in a peculiar light by the words of the dying man. Prolonged thinking brought only wider distraction, and the unhappy father determined to question his daughter, depending on the close sympathy between them to bring the whole truth from her.

It was some time, however, before he could find the opportunity. Mr. Blanchard had removed his son to his home and had retained Dr. Osborne to attend him. When the surgeon had done all that was possible, he went to his home and sought his daughter. But she could not be found.

After nearly crying her heart out upon her return from Armour's office, she got up, brought herself under control, and then realized that she had been treated shamefully by the man whom she loved above all others in the world. It was easy for her grief to become shame and her shame anger. It was not possible for her yet to think seriously upon any plan that might bring suffering or ruin to her lover; but it was within her power to work serious mischief to some mysterious woman who had come between her and him, and this was a matter to be attended to. Accordingly she cleared up her face, made herself very bright and pretty, and went at once to consult the chief of police.

That functionary was vastly surprised so see her. He had been given a full report of the scene at the receiving hospital, and when he saw the girl enter his office looking so bright, confident, and handsome, and announce her name and mission, he was sorely perplexed. In truth, Chief Holloway had certain ideas which would have given Miss Agnes discomfort if she had known of their existence.

"I have come to ask you, Mr. Holloway," she said, "if you have made any discoveries concerning the shooting of Mr. Blanchard."

The officer, somewhat taken aback by her directness, tried, after a heavy fashion, to cover his position under some remarks in which discretion was outlined as a duty. "But this is rather a singular question from you, Miss Osborne, considering that you yourself are supposed to know all about the matter."

The very boldness and brutality of the assault served an excellent purpose; for the girl, not dreaming that her talk with young Blanchard had taken wings, or that any one suspected her of knowledge, was shocked with surprise.

"What makes you think that?" she quickly asked.

This put him in command of the situation, for he felt his power.

"Your conversation with young Blanchard showed that both you and he know all about it, and then, after you left him you went to see Dr. Armour, who also appears to be pretty badly mixed up in the whole affair."

All this came like a whirlwind, and badly frightened the girl.

"Now," resumed Holloway, "although you have come ostensibly to make inquiries, I think your ultimate purpose was to give some very important information. I should be pleased to hear it."

Agnes caught her breath. "How can I know anything?" she asked, realizing that her time had come, but with a rush that unnerved her; "Mr. Blanchard spoke in a rambling way."

"But he was not as evasive as you are at this moment."

"Evasive? Really, sir – " "This is no time for by-play." sternly interrupted the officer; "no doubt you understand that you yourself are in a very peculiar position. If what you know would endanger your own safety by your telling it, I can easily understand your feelings."

The sting was felt, but the girl rallied and gave this opinion:

"You said something just now that makes me think you suspect Dr. Armour of having a guilty knowledge of the affair. If you mean by that to charge him with the crime, you are entirely in error."

"But you are careful not to deny that he knows something of importance. Why do you not say openly that you and Armour know who fired the shot, and that you two, possibly for prudential reasons, are doing all you can to conceal your knowledge and shield the criminal?"

The very brutality and directness of the question roused the inmost nature of the girl. With scarlet face and flashing eyes she said:

"If you will come with me, I will show you the murderer."

This was a windfall that Holloway had not dared to hope for. He promptly followed Agnes.

When they had reached the street, she said:

"It will be necessary to see Dr. Armour first, and I think he is at Mr. Blanchard's. We will go there first."

"As you please."

They found both Dr. Amour and Dr. Osborne at the young man's house. The two physicians – the father and the lover – were vastly surprised so see Agnes and the chief of police walk in together. For her part, Agnes felt so guilty that she could not bear to look Armour full in the face.

She felt that a wild jealousy had led her so take a desperate and dangerous step, the end of which she could not foresee. But did her lover really deserve to be spared? Had he not deceived her shamefully? The young man felt that a high barrier had come between him and Agnes, and hence he had nothing to say to her. Holloway readily saw that a heavy constraint rested upon them both, and it appeared, in his eyes, an important affair.

"Agnes," said her father, taking her by the hand, and looking her anxiously in the eyes, "where have you been?"

"To see Mr. Holloway, father."

"For what purpose?"

"To learn if he had discovered anything."

This was not the place for pressing the matter, and so her father asked her no more questions.

There was a moment of general embarrassment among the four persons in the room, and it was broken by the chief, who asked that in the cause of justice Miss Osborne be permitted to repeat the experiment of inserting her finger in the wound. With surprising alacrity both the physicians objected, saying that the wound had been dressed, that the sufferer was then very low from shock, and that such an experiment would likely have a fatal issue. Holloway smiled in a peculiar manner, and, looking steadily at Armour, added:

"I hardly expected that you would consent."

This thrust cut the young man to the quick, and he shot a look at Agnes that revealed his suspicion of her hand in the policy of the officer.

"Of course I have no desire to increase the young man's danger," remarked Holloway; "but the result of the former experiment was so important that I deemed it advisable to repeat it if possible. However, I think it is hardly necessary. As soon as I had learned all the particulars of that experiment, I laid them before a prominent physician of this city, and requested his written opinion concerning them. I think this is the proper time to inform you concerning it, for several reasons, which will appear later."

Thereupon Holloway read an ingenious paper, only a short extract from which can be set forth here. It is as follows:

"Admitting a wide latitude for deception on the part of the young woman, and the possibility of error in your account, the whole affair seems preposterous and not worthy of serious attention. But we shall treat it, not as a fact, but as a hypothetical case." (The hypothesis was here stated in agreement with the reported facts, and this explanation followed:) "The bullet was small, and hence the laceration of the brain matter was not extensive nor the primary shock very great. The unconsciousness observed apparently resulted from the severing of the nerves ramifying throughout the brain and from the rupturing of the innumerable chains of brain-cells in the path of the bullet. These lacerations, by destroying the continuity of the brain texture, disorganized the mind by interrupting the coordination of its functions.

"If, now, some plan could have been devised for bringing together the severed ends of tissue in such a manner as would permit of their resuming theft normal occupation of transmitting molecular activity, there is a rare possibility that its employment would have restored consciousness. By a very singular accident, the young woman may have performed that service when she inserted her finger deep into the brain; but, in order for this result to have been accomplished, a most extraordinary series of events must have occurred."

"The finger is a sensitive member, from the fact that it contains so large a number of nerves."

"These nerves, called peripheral, terminate under a thin cuticle, through which sensation is easily experienced. When her finger was inserted in the brain tissue, her nerve-ends came approximately in contact with the severed nerves of the brain over the entire field of laceration."

"Thus the mechanical condition of nerve-continuity was restored in the brain of the wounded man, and consciousness was the result."

"But it is evident that the molecular transmission did not occur directly through her finger."

"That was not possible, for the reason that her nerves do not run straight through her finger from one side to the other. If we should trace one of these nerves, we should find that, starting at the termination in the finger, it runs up the arm into the brain. A sensation, starting from the end and going to the brain, would there meet and be assimilated by a large number of other sensations, this being the result of coordination. The brain would then decide what action to take, and then would direct the efferent, or outrunning, nerves to move the muscles with a definite purpose. It is clear, then, that the movement of sensation through the wounded man's brain tissue, after the restoration of continuity, must have become communicated to the nervous system of the woman."

"In other words, no sensation could pass through his brain without passing through hers also. In this way, their two brains would act largely as one, and the active thoughts of one would be known to the other. By this sort of reasoning we may account for the fact that, although the two persons were strangers to each other, mutual recognition came when the knowledge of both became the possession of each. Hence we must infer that the young woman knows as much concerning the person who did the shooting as does the wounded man himself?"

The effect of this extraordinary document can hardly be imagined. From Dr. Osborne it lifted a load that was likely to crush him. But why had not his daughter been candid with him? Now that there no longer could be a fair suspicion that she had any criminal association with the crime, why had she acted in so strange a manner?

Armour's thoughts took a very different turn. His pallor increased until it became alarming, and his knees were unsteady from weakness. The man's agony was so painfully visible that Agnes felt a fearful dread for the end that must come.

The immediate result of all this was that the three men fixed a steady gaze upon her, in which was a commingling of peculiar motives and sensations.

"Miss Osborne," finally said Holloway, "this scientific report leads us to believe that you are fully aware of the identity of the one who fired the shot. In corroboration of these conclusions, you have confessed your knowledge by offering your services to point out the murderer to me. Will you be so kind as to keep your promise?"

All that was womanly in the girl found cause both for alarm and encouragement in this situation. Against her sense of wrong weighed that of tenderness and affection. She found courage to look Armour squarely in the face, hoping to receive some sign that might guide her; but she found – as she read his expression – only contempt and defiance struggling through the cloud of anguish which sat upon him.

"I will keep my promise," she said, with much firmness; "we will now go to Dr. Armour's office."

Besides becoming somewhat more rigid, as though bracing himself to meet some fearful ordeal, Armour betrayed no emotion. Dr. Osborne appeared to be overcome with astonishment and anxiety. Chief Holloway only smiled.

These four went at once to Armour's office in utter silence, each feeling the imminence of a catastrophe. The young physician admitted them into the outer room, and then closed the door.

With great abruptness, he then asked this question:

"Will some one be kind enough to explain the object of this visitation?"

Holloway was on the point of speaking, but Agnes stepped before him, and, looking Armour firmly in the face, said:

"I believe that the person who committed this crime is concealed in your consultation-room. If I am wrong, heaven will punish me as I deserve. So far as I am able to discover, no reason exists why I should pretend to deny the knowledge which I have. The murderer is a woman, and you are concealing and shielding her in that room."

Armour, though pale as death, did not flinch before this accusation. On the contrary, his chest expanded, his eyes flashed, and, with head thrown back, he said: "It was a woman who did the shooting, as I now believe, and it is true that she at this moment is kept in concealment by me in my inner office. I had hoped to be able to conceal her act from the world, for if ever there was an occasion for the exercise of the noblest human traits, it is in the case before us. Let me tell you something – you who mistake suspicion for skill in unearthing crime, and you who are moved by even less worthy motives – crime can not exist in the absence of accountability. Has it occurred to you to imagine that this woman may not have been responsible for her act? Do you know what an epileptic fit is? Surely you do, Dr. Osborne. You are familiar with the strange forms which this disease may take. You know that the sweetest natures are at times wholly perverted by it; that its manifestations are complex and obscure; that sometimes, instead of the violent spasms with which we are all familiar the malady takes the form of mental and physical activity, in which we find an impulse to commit extraordinary acts as the result of monstrous misconceptions. When this condition occurs, all the principles of the victim's nature may be wholly eclipsed, conscience entirely suppressed, and the power to discriminate between right and wrong completely lost. After the attack has passed, there remains no recollection of what was done during its continuance.

"I inform you – and I am able to prove my assertion – that the woman who shot my dearest friend is now in my inner office; that she came to me from a distant city only yesterday to be treated for this very malady; that very soon after her arrival, I informed her, as was my duty and pleasure, that I was engaged to marry a very charming and kind-hearted young lady. It is a breach of delicate confidence on my part to inform you that, in spite of a brave effort to appear glad for my good fortune, she could not conceal a certain unhappiness which I know was perfectly natural, but it is my duty now to tell you everything. I now know that the sorrow which my news caused her brought on an attack of what is known as masked epilepsy, to which she is subject. The thing uppermost in her mind was that some one was dearer to me than she was; although normally a woman of unexampled sweetness and goodness, she determined, in her condition of temporary insanity, to kill that person. I need not inform you that she most have started out with the clear purpose of killing the young lady to whom I was affianced. But she knew, also, that young Blanchard was my dearest friend, and, in her wild mental condition, she happened to find him fast, and she fired into his brain the bullet that was intended for another."

The young man paused awhile, but he did not cast a glance at Agnes, who, feeling unaccountably faint as these strange revelations were made, had sunk helpless upon a chair "Ms. Holloway," resumed Armour, "I ask your promise that you will not arrest this woman now, but that you take proper steps to verify my assertions; and as she has recovered from her attack, and has no recollection whatever of the tragedy, you say nothing to her about it now, and that you never mention it to a soul if you find that what I have told you is true.

"I cheerfully give those two promises," said Holloway.

"Then," said Armour, "I will present the lady to you."

With that he went to the door of the inner room, unlocked it, and stepped within. In the next moment he returned, supporting on his arm a pale, sweet-faced, beautiful woman of fifty, in whose sad and gentle face was no trace of the fearful thing she had done. Armour, with his head thrown hack and glowing with all the pride of a gentleman, thus presented her:

"Miss Osborne and gentlemen, I have the honor to make you acquainted with my mother."